INNOCENCE LOST

Ghostspeaker Chronicles Book 1

PATTY JANSEN

Capricornica Publications

GET FREE EBOOKS

Visit pattyjansen.com
to sign up for Patty's mailing list. You get four series starter
ebooks for free!

CHAPTER 1

JOHANNA SASHAYED down the church aisle towards the open doors that beckoned her to freedom. Her clogs clonked on the wooden floor, clop-clop-clop. With each sway of her hips, her skirts swished around her ankles, and her plait swung over her back, free of the bonnet.

Outrageous. Improper.

Poor girl, needs a mother. Look at her clothes. As if her father can't afford anything better. He's giving her far too much freedom.

She knew the whispers of the merchants' wives, the not-quite-nobles and other hangers-on of the Saardam gentry, and all the others in the pews. She knew the rules of the church about women, *that they should dress modestly and not show any exuberance or draw attention to themselves.*

There would be hell to pay for this later, but today, she didn't care.

On second thoughts, coming to church wearing her clogs instead of her proper shoes was probably not her smartest idea ever. But she didn't want to get her best shoes dirty. Of course she had a second-best pair of shoes, but even her second best pair of shoes was too good for the markets, where farmers cast their scraps on the ground and their pigs and cows and chickens left their business, and where the cobbles were always covered in slimy mud.

Indeed, the daughter of a merchant who hoped to attain noble status wasn't supposed to go to the markets. One had *servants* for the purpose.

Not that she cared about that either. Because, for once, the weather gods smiled on Saardam, bringing out the colours, the paint on the merchants' houses, the red of the roofs, the blue water in the canals, the brilliant green of the leaves on the trees, the yellow of the cheeses on the market stalls, the blue and white shirts of the cheese sellers. Had she ever noticed how many weeds grew between the pavers in the street and how brightly yellow the dandelions bloomed? Did she remember how blue the sky was and how white the clouds?

She stopped at the church door, drinking it in.

She called it *freedom,* now that the boring part of the day was done.

The sunlight was kind even to Nellie, with wisps of flaxen hair peeking out from under her oh-so-proper bonnet. Her eyes were clear and blue and her skin was like the velvet bottom of the neighbour's baby, so much prettier than Johanna's. Those cheeks now flushed with red as she caught up with Johanna at the church doors, bowing and apologising to all those who had nothing better to do than complain.

She whispered, "Mistress Johanna, you aren't wearing your proper shoes."

"Aren't I?" Johanna lifted up the hem of her skirt, letting the sunlight fall on her clogs. Pretty ones, these were, too, with painted patterns and made from willow wood that sang its stories to her whenever she wore them. Happy stories, of fat cows, green pastures, and peace.

"Your shoes were in your room. I put them there this morning."

"Oh. I must have missed them."

She clonked down the church steps, clop-clop-clop on the wood. Clop-clop-clop down the new stairs of the new entrance porch with its Lurezian woodwork and stained glass windows. Clop-clop-clop onto the cobbled street.

See me? I'm wearing my clogs to church. If there is any such thing as the Triune—which I doubt—He will love me or hate me with my clogs just as much as with my shoes.

"Come, let's go!"

Nellie sighed and rolled her eyes. She did that a lot lately.

Frivolous, they called Johanna, and said she needed a man. But have you ever noticed how marriage takes the life out of a woman's eyes?

She slid into the crowds of the markets, the servants, shopkeepers and common people buying their daily needs: bread, butter and cheese; potatoes, fish and—shudder—cabbage.

"Good day Mistress Johanna, good day, Nellie," said Leo Mustermans, standing behind his stall. He wore his Market Day best, a hose that was grey and less patched than what he usually wore when lugging cheeses from the sloops in the harbour. He did well enough; under his golden hair he had a round face, now sweaty and squinting into the sunlight.

"Beautiful day today," Johanna said. "The cheese will be good this summer."

"That, it will be, Mistress Johanna. Though the cheese will get sweaty if the breeze doesn't pick up."

She laughed. She wanted to say, *Just like you* but Leo would laugh, because he was that kind of man, and others would know what she'd said and next thing *that* would be added to her list of recent sins.

"It's good quality cheese, the kind the Estlanders like." He looked like he wanted to add something about Johanna's father buying his cheese and selling it to Estland, but he didn't. She was a frivolous *girl* after all and one couldn't possibly discuss business with a girl. Fancy that.

Then he asked, "You're all excited for the king's ball?"

Johanna laughed but her good mood fled the instant he mentioned the word "ball". Why did they always have to ask about that? As if it were the only thing that mattered for a young woman in Saardam: to be invited to the royal ball. She said through clenched teeth, "Our family is not important enough to go to the ball."

"I'm sorry to hear that."

"Don't be, because I don't want to go."

"But you should be invited, Mistress Johanna. You'd be pretty enough to turn all the noble boys' heads, and brainy enough to outsmart them all."

She laughed, the sound again hollow. "Thanks for the flattery, Leo, but no thanks. I'm glad I don't have to go." It was not like the noble boys *wanted* brainy girls.

"It's a pity. The rumour goes that the king will announce a surprise for the citizens of Saardam."

Johanna had heard that, too, whispered to her by the wood of the pews in the church. She stifled a wave of suspicion and dread. Last year, the king's surprise had been his donation of the statue of the Triune to the Church. The thing was so big that it had come on a river sloop pulled by two full teams of sea cows all the way from Lurezia. The blocks of the statue had to be dismantled even further before they fitted through the church door.

She hoped the surprise would be nowhere as extravagant as that. And that it would be something that people could use. She heard the Burovian king had paid for a new concert hall, and that Lurezia now had a building dedicated to the study of the skies. Why couldn't King Nicholaos give something like that? "I'm sure we'll hear about it soon enough."

"That is true. We will, Mistress Johanna." He nodded. "Have a nice day."

"A nice day to you, too."

She walked away from the stall, running her fingers over the wooden planks of the trestles groaning under the weight of his cheeses, big, fat yellow ones. The willow wood brought images of grazing cows and green fields to her mind—buttercups and dandelions, and stacks of drying hay.

"He *is* right, you know," Nellie said in a soft voice once they were in the next aisle.

"What?" Johanna frowned at her, still thinking of green meadows and fat cows.

"You *should* be invited to the ball. Your father is important enough. He's certainly wealthy enough."

"Oh, pfaw, Nellie. He's a merchant. Haven't you noticed how much the nobles get out of their way to put us in our place? I'm glad I don't have to go and that's the truth of it. Do you see me dancing and twirling in frilly dresses? Do you see me walking up the steps to the palace with half of Saardam gawking at me and gossiping about what I'm wearing? I can just about hear their voices already: 'She *is* very coarse, isn't she?' and 'Goodness me, who did her hair?' or '*What* is she wearing?'"

"They are doing that already." Nellie glared pointedly at Johanna's clogs.

Yes, she got the point.

Clearly scenting blood, Nellie stuck her nose in the air. "It would be a good opportunity to show that you're a real lady. It's not too late for you to find a good husband—"

"Nellie, have you noticed that as soon as a woman gets married, she dresses 'proper' and suddenly loses her youth and her sense of fun? Well, I have no intention of becoming like that."

"You can still be a fun person when you're married."

"Show me a woman who managed that, and I will believe it."

She glared at Nellie and Nellie glared back.

In her eyes Johanna saw the frustration of years of waiting, the embarrassment of watching her mistress do things that made her cringe. Johanna's father employed Nellie as a personal maid and companion, but she wanted to be the maid of a household, a servant to the man Johanna was yet to marry, and a governess to the children Johanna didn't have.

You're twenty-four, mistress. It is beyond time that you were married.

Why did discussions always come back to that old subject?

It was getting very tiresome.

She continued from stall to stall, across the cobbled pavement, sliding her hands over the wood and hearing in the wood's essence the conversations of men who had put out the trestles early this morning, the voices of the merchants as they arrived, the gossip, the people who were always late paying, the liars and cheats, who married whom, who cheated with whom, that sort of thing. She listened to the talk of merchants, about accounts, about imports, the sort of news she would relay to her father.

Then Johanna came around a corner and found a stall with stacks of baskets of the type that were woven from willow twigs. Her heart leapt. Loesie was here.

Johanna hadn't seen Loesie since the pale beginning of spring. She lived with her grandmother on the flood plains of the Saar River that looped around Saarland to form the northern border with the kingdom of Estland and the eastern border with the barony of Gelre.

Nellie had seen Loesie, too, because she touched Johanna's arm. "Please, Mistress Johanna, it's time to—"

"I need a basket for my embroidery things."

"But you hardly ever do embroidery, Mistress Johanna."

"That's why I need a basket—to keep it out of my way."

"But you have a room full of baskets. A basket for your wool, a basket for your laundry, a basket for your winter blankets . . ." She counted on her fingers. "I could scarce find room for another one."

"I am sure you can find one that is broken."

Johanna progressed to the stall, Nellie hobbling behind her, protesting that Johanna never broke any baskets. She felt sorry for Nellie; only sometimes, though. On second thoughts, Nellie was a nice girl, but she really needed to stand up for herself more, even against her mistress. Especially against her mistress, because she took advantage of it.

Having felt Johanna approach, as Johanna knew Loesie would, Loesie rose from behind a pile of baskets.

And there the day turned not-so-very-good at all.

The young woman in the stall was no longer the one Johanna knew as her friend, no longer the vivid, laughing, large-eyed creature that people in town called a witch when they thought Johanna wasn't listening. No longer the figure that inspired fear in Nellie and the ship's boys who sneaked around trying to steal from the stalls.

This pale shell of her friend was like a ghost. Her mist-grey eyes were wide, her skin so pale it was almost translucent. A black dress hung off bony shoulders, and a black scarf covered her limp, grey-brown hair.

As Loesie recognised Johanna, her face split into a grin, but it was more like a grimace. Her cheeks were death-pale.

Johanna ran to her, simultaneously horrified and revolted. "Loesie! What happened to you?"

Her arms closed around Loesie's shoulders, and at the

same time, a shudder of cold went through her. There was no meat on Loesie's bones at all. "A sickness? Death in the family?"

Loesie only looked at Johanna.

"What happened, Loesie? Where is your grandmother?" But it was clear that she had come alone. There were not as many baskets as usual and the stall was rather messy.

Loesie's lips opened, but her mouth made only a kind of *ghghghgh* noise from the back of her throat. She lifted her hand up to her neck. It sounded like she had a turnip stuck down there.

"You can't speak?"

She nodded.

"You have a disease?"

She shook her head. Her eyes bore a glazed expression, as one—Johanna shivered—one touched by magic.

Of course the Shepherd in church said there was no magic, and that's what the people wanted to believe. The Church had no control over magic, because magic flows where magic goes, in the wood of the willow trees, in the wind and in the water. Magic didn't happen for everyone, and certainly didn't answer to priests and their prayers.

So magic or no, Johanna knew not what else to call it, but it hovered in Loesie's eyes sure as she could hear willow wood speak.

Johanna dug under her apron, trying not to notice how thin Loesie was and how ill her grandmother's dress fitted her, and how her skin had paled until it looked like she was a corpse that had floated in the water for days. She took a bag of biscuits out of her pocket and slipped it into Loesie's hands. She scrunched open the paper.

"Go on then, eat them. They're good. Koby made them."

With her bone-thin fingers, Loesie broke a piece off a biscuit and popped in her mouth. She closed her eyes as she chewed, then she smiled. Johanna put her hand on Loesie's shoulder. "Tonight you should sleep in Father's sea-cow barn. You'll be warm there. I'll bring you some food, right?"

She nodded.

From the corner of her eye, Johanna could see Nellie fidgeting.

Yes, yes, I know I came here to buy a basket. Let's choose a basket, then.

She ran her fingers over the rim of a coarsely-woven laundry basket. The stripped willow twigs made her skin tingle. She heard laughter, sloshing of water around a boat, the voices of a young man and a young woman. She pulled away and reached for another basket. Those twigs gave her no more than the soft lowing of cows. The next thing, a foot-stool made from willow twigs, contained a male voice, which said, "You know, one day in spring a flood will come and all this land will be under water."

A boy responded, "Can't we stop it?"

"No, son, it needs to happen. It's part of life."

Johanna withdrew her fingers. She'd heard all these voices before. They came from twigs cut from willows around town.

Loesie rummaged under her table and pulled out a few more baskets, none of which were in the shape of anything that Johanna could remotely use for storing embroidery.

She glanced over her shoulder at Nellie, who scrunched her hands up before her, white-knuckled, and who was studiously avoiding gazes from genteel citizens, glances that said, *You should tell your mistress not to involve herself with such questionable people.* Poor Nellie.

Then Loesie pulled a square basket that had been at the bottom of the pile and held it out to Johanna, uttering more *ghghghgh* sounds.

"For me?"

She nodded, her eyes vivid.

The moment Johanna touched the woven twigs, she heard the most bloodcurdling scream she had ever heard in her life. A woman. It was night and the pale moonlight wasn't strong enough to show what was happening. There were men's voices, too, rough and . . . foreign. The sound of galloping hooves, and a low, guttural, demonic roar. Some kind of creature bounded through tall grass. All Johanna saw was a silhouette, pushing aside tall grass and leaves that occasionally reflected the moonlight like silver. The creature ran flat-footed, was long-haired, and had small, rounded ears and a long snout, like a hunting dog, except it was much bigger than that.

She dropped the basket, goose bumps crawling over her arms. "Where . . ." She gulped for air. "Where did this wood come from?"

Loesie thudded her hand on her chest.

"You cut it?"

She nodded.

If she cut it, it must come from somewhere close to her grandmother's farm. Johanna bent to pick up the basket, and used her apron to touch the wood. The messages in the wood faded the more people touched it.

Did that poor screaming woman survive? What was that dreadful roar? What was that creature? Willow tales were always true. If that's what the tree had seen, then that was how it had happened.

"Loesie—was this at your grandmother's farm?"

She nodded and mimicked fighting.

"They're bandits? Coming into Saarland?"

She nodded again and then formed her hands into claws and mimicked a roar.

"And demons?"

Loesie nodded again.

Except the kingdom of Saarland had been at peace for

many years. There had not been any marauding bands of invaders for a long time. Certainly not magical ones.

Johanna wanted to set the basket down, but Loesie gestured for her to keep it and pointed across the marketplace.

"You want me to leave?"

"*Ghghghghgh!*" She shook her head and pointed more strenuously.

Nellie reminded Johanna, "We should be on our way, Mistress Johanna. We have to be back for midday—"

"Cowpats, Nellie, we have plenty of time."

Nellie's cheeks darkened. "Mistress Johanna. You shouldn't say such . . . things. And in the marketplace, too, where everyone can hear it, mind you. What is your father going to say when he hears—"

"Stop it, Nellie, before I say any worse words. My friend needs help. That's much more important than what people think of me."

Then, spotting the crest of Saardam above the entrance to the council chambers, she realised what Loesie had been trying to say. "You want me to tell someone, like the mayor?"

She nodded, her eyes wide, while she gripped Johanna's arm. "*Ghghghgh!*"

"Yes, I will." Though what she would tell a mayor who went to church every day and didn't believe in magic she didn't know. She could just about see the man's face, over his hideous ruffled collar. *The wood told you there are bands of rogues about?* "If I'm to make a convincing story, I need to know who these men are and where they are now."

Loesie made a sweeping motion with her hand.

"Everywhere?"

She nodded.

Johanna looked at the peaceful market scenes, the cheese

merchants, the fabric sellers, the turnip farmers, all people she knew reasonably well. No one she didn't.

"Here?"

Loesie made a sound of frustration. "Ghghghghgh!"

"In the city?"

Loesie pulled her arm again, placing her hand flat on her chest. Then she pointed at Johanna.

"Yes, I promise I'll tell someone."

CHAPTER 2

WHATEVER HAPPENED to the nice day?

Johanna left the markets with no idea what she was going to do about the promise she'd made to Loesie. She couldn't just walk into the mayor's office and tell him about the magic warning.

The mayor went to church and took the Shepherd's teaching *very* seriously. A few weeks ago in church, the Shepherd Romulus had given a sermon that condemned magic in the strongest possible words. Johanna could still hear his voice. *There are those who adhere to the dark crafts of old, from quacks who tell the people lies about treatments that do not work, and fortune-tellers who take your money for deceit and extortion, to those who try to do evil. They tell you they see things on the wind or in the wood. These are lies. At best, the dark crafts are a fallacy. At worst, they are evil.*

He let his words echo through the church.

Then there are those, at the pinnacle of all evil, who willingly engage in the black arts that are the domain of the Lord of Fire. Those who seek to possess other people, those who speak to ghosts, and worst of all, those who try to raise the dead.

A kind of shudder had gone through the congregation at those words.

Johanna remembered sitting in her pew with her hands clamped between her knees, feeling like the Triune itself would burst through the ceiling of the church and point a great shining light at her. A big voice would boom through the church, *Here is a sinner and a witch and yet she sits in our church every day and she shares our meals. Who knows what she reads about you when she runs her hand over your dining table?*

It was at times like this that her father's words haunted her: that she didn't belong in this church—which she knew because she didn't really believe in the Triune—and that she should stop going to it.

But the church was useful. The benches made of willow wood were full of stories, which they released to her at the touch of her hands. They taught her many things she would never have known otherwise.

And everyone went to church. Everyone of her age at least. It was new, it was a good thing for the citizens, because the Verses taught that people should be sensible, compassionate, honest and frugal, all things that the Lurezian culture that had gripped the nobles of the city was not. Of course the nobles and those who wanted to be nobles disliked the Church's teachings against blatant displays of wealth.

There was just that little problem about magic and the way the Shepherd portrayed all magic as black and evil. One day, Johanna had told herself, she was going to show the Church that magic was mostly used for good. But that day hadn't come yet and each day the Church's teachings against magic intensified.

Increasing numbers of people, like the mayor, believed in the evil of magic. That was because many had never seen it.

Many, many people couldn't see things in willow wood, or hear voices on the wind, and therefore, to these people, this magic was something dark and evil. They liked what the Shepherd said about magic: that it was the mark of the Lord of Fire and those who practiced it were disciples of that evil force.

For Johanna, there was no right or wrong about magic. Magic just was. The wood showed her what the wood had seen. It re-played those images until the magic ran out. There was nothing evil about it, nothing that she could control. The magic was in the wood. She was simply there to see it.

But because the Church and the Shepherd had become popular—and because the king went to church—it meant that if she needed to warn people, there was no way that she could do so with Loesie's story alone.

She couldn't tell anyone of the bloodcurdling scream from that woman or the demons, because she couldn't explain how she had seen them.

A plain warning that *some people crossed the river* would not bother anyone, because people in the border regions crossed the river all the time. Yet if Johanna spoke of the demons, they'd say that this was a hallucination by an unstable woman, unmarried and *frivolous*. The Church would consider *her* evil, too.

But she knew what the wood had shown her was true.

Who could these invaders be?

Saarland had been at peace for longer than Father had been alive.

She didn't *think* the royal family had offended anyone. They preferred trade with the neighbouring countries. Father's sloops, the *Lady Sara* and *Lady Davida* and the smaller ones, went up and down the river all the time. Father met with the Estlanders at Aroden castle and went as far as the rapids where the Saar River came down from the moun-tains in Westfalia, far beyond the borders even of Gelre. He'd never said anything about threats or bandits. It just made no sense.

There was only one thing to do: she needed to find out if someone else had seen anything.

Johanna said to Nellie, "You go ahead. Tell my father I'll be home soon."

"But Mistress, what are you going to do? It's almost midday." And midday was dinner and heaven forbid if she was late for that, even if only with her own father. *Do you ever not think about what's proper, Nellie?*

"I won't be long. There is something I have to do right now."

"Your father will be so angry if you're late. And what with you wearing your clogs to church—"

"Please, Nellie." Johanna held up her hands.

"Your father wants me to keep you—"

"Out of mischief and on the right path, yes. I'm not going to do anything silly. I just need to talk to someone."

Nellie glared at her and an unspoken warning hung between them.

It had something to do with the time last month that Johanna had borrowed a looking glass and wanted to see how the Moon would take a bite out of the Sun, as Jan Dieckens, who was the lighthouse keeper but who spent a lot of time looking at the stars, said.

But it happened at dusk and the sun was so low that Johanna couldn't see it from her bedroom widow, or the garden, so she'd climbed up on the roof through the attic window in the drying room. Before going out there, she had taken off her dress because it was too cumbersome for climbing on roofs, right?

But it so happened that her father had wanted to see her, and not finding her in her room, he had asked the servants, and none of them knew where she was. Then they all started looking, and getting more concerned until the gardener—a man no less—found her on the roof wearing only her drawers. What a scandal that had been!

"Please yourself, Nellie. You can go home, or you can come with me, but I am going. And the sooner I go, the quicker I'll be back." She turned and walked away.

Nellie ran after her. "Where are you going?" The words *to the roof in your drawers?* hung in her voice.

"To Father's office."

Nellie's eyes widened. Apparently she had expected something entirely different. Some of the tension went out of her posture.

The merchant office of the Brouwer spice merchants was along the harbour, in one of the stately buildings on the quay. The front window looked out over the harbour, and the ships, the sails, the masts and the activity that came with the many different kinds of ships.

There were big sailing vessels that went over the ocean, which went to places as far as the Horn and beyond, and brought back exotic spices and silks. There were the trusty river barges such as Johanna's father owned, which lay, ugly and plain, side-by-side in the glittering water of the harbour. A ship's boy was jumping from one boat to the other. A couple of quay workers were unloading fat cheeses onto a cart. With their greenish hue, they were Estlander cheeses, made from sheep's milk. That was what Father did: he took the exotic spices and silks to the inland cities of the east, and brought back their cheeses and dainty cabbage sprouts. He'd said not long ago that the company had enough money to invest in a seafaring vessel, but no one would dream of setting sail without guards to protect the vessel against pirates on the open ocean, and mercenaries did not work for common citizens. And the nobles wouldn't accept Father as one of them.

It was all very silly and frustrating.

A few herder boys in rowing boats were taking a group of sea cows across to the barns on the other side of the harbour. The sunlight glistened on the animals' hairy backs. They could probably already smell the cabbages and carrots in the water. The Brouwer Company's barn was somewhere amongst the boathouses perched on stilts over the water. This was where Loesie would sleep. Johanna would come back tonight and check on her.

As she squinted into the light, she noticed that there was an unusual sloop in the harbour. With its dark-painted sides and large cabin, with real glass windows and red curtains, it didn't look like a cargo ship. In fact, it looked like some rich person's private ship.

A few men sat on the deck of the *Lady Sara,* the Brouwer Company's flagship, smoking and drinking coffee, and waved as Johanna passed.

"Good morning, Mistress Johanna."

She stopped. "Good morning, Adrian. How's business?"

"We delivered the cheese to the Hendricksen warehouse. The *Lady Davida* should be back tomorrow with the wheat."

"Make sure the hold gets cleaned out properly. The *Lady Davida* will be taking a shipment of fine food to Estland, and I'm sure Lord Aroden won't like finding weevils in his biscuits."

"Sure, Mistress Johanna." Adrian snorted, no doubt thinking of *that* weevil incident.

She nodded at the black barge. "Do you know who that ship belongs to?"

"The black one?"

"Yes. Whose is it?"

"Don't know, Mistress, but I wager it's someone important. They arrived last night and there was a big to-do with folk on horses and carriages. All of it after dark, mind. Didn't see who came in, but it musta been important. Master

Willems saw them too and said they might be guests for the royal family."

Oh, that dratted ball again. Now there were important *foreign* guests, huh? Wonder what outrageous things they would be wearing?

Pardon the sarcasm.

She looked at the boat and its immaculate shiny deck and she couldn't begin to figure who this important person would be. She would have recognised the Estlander flag if they were people from the Estlander royal family. But it wasn't the Estlander family standard. It was a blue flag with a small yellow emblem in it that depicted something complicated, like a flower or a frilled dragon, but was too far away for her to see.

"What company does that flag belong to?"

He shrugged. "Something Burovian. Heard a rumour that it belonged to some religious order's sanatorium. Dunno if that's true, mind . . ."

That didn't sit well with her. The Church—a religious order—a sanatorium. People from a Burovian religious order invited to the ball? King Nicholaos had become so obsessed with religion recently—religion which forbade magic. Magic, which she could not help having. Church, which she attended because everyone did, but where she didn't completely feel at ease.

She shivered. "Thank you, Adrian."

He waved and she continued on to the office of the Brouwer Company. The bells above the door clanged as she stepped inside, onto the familiar wooden floor where she'd played as a child, the familiar desk, now empty, where the office clerk usually sat, and the shelves with samples on the back wall. Even the smell was familiar. Tobacco, curry, nutmeg, cinnamon.

Nellie followed her and closed the door, shutting out the harbour sounds.

Master Willems, fresh-faced and red-cheeked, in black over-dress and white ruffled shirt, came out of the door to Father's office.

"Good morning Mistress Johanna. Good morning, Nellie."

It was still morning. Only just.

He must have been ready to go out to the Church midday service because he held a thumbed copy of the Book of the Triune in his hands. He was Reader at church and would stand to the side of the altar and read out passages of the Verses.

"I haven't finished the Pietersen account yet," he said. "I'm sorry, I know I promised your father but I've been—"

"I didn't come for the Pietersen account. I want to talk to you."

"Oh?" He raised one blond eyebrow. One corner of his mouth quivered. He wasn't handsome, exactly, but trust-worthy and dependable. If it hadn't been for his piousness, Johanna might even have liked him. "Me? Well, Mistress Johanna, I'm not sure that I—" He looked more puzzled now.

"It's about the wind."

"What wind?"

His face went blank, but by the way he gripped the edge of the table, Johanna figured he knew what this was about. He looked from her to Nellie, as if he wanted to say, *how much does she know?* and then jerked his head at the back office. They went inside, leaving Nellie in the front room.

Inside, by the hearth, big velvet-covered chairs took up most of the space. Account books lay in tottering piles on the heavy wooden desk in the corner. This used to be her father's desk, but her father hardly came in anymore, preferring to do his work from the comfort of his chair by the fire at home.

The air in the room smelled of fresh tobacco and an array of spices that were laid out on the table. He must have had a visiting buyer this morning.

Johanna sat down in one of the chairs, Master Willems in the other, smoothing the folds of his robe. He still held the Book of the Triune, and clutched it to his chest, nervously.

They sat there in silence for an uncomfortable moment before Johanna asked, "Have you seen anything on the wind lately, Master Willems?"

He froze, the book of the Triune in his hand. She had never spoken of magic, much less that she knew he could read wind magic from the way he stood at the end of the pier, letting the wind buffet him.

He pursed his lips, and eyes looked at her as if she was something disgusting washed up on the shore. "Of what do you speak, Mistress Johanna?"

He knew very well of what she spoke.

Johanna spoke in a low voice. "This can stay between us. You and I both know I have no great love for people who sow fear amongst the citizens for something they have no control over. The magic is in the wood and in the water and the wind. We do a lot of good with it. To blame those who can see it is not fair, and I cannot believe that any benevolent deity would agree to shame law-abiding citizens."

He gulped a few times.

She continued, "I do not care what you believe privately, but for the safety of our country, tell me if you've seen anything."

"Why . . . why should I have seen something . . . if I could see . . . things on the wind?" He wiped sweat from his upper lip.

Johanna put her newest basket on the table.

"Touch the willow wood, Master Willems. Can you tell me if you see anything?"

He did, and shook his head. "Do you see something. . . ?" His voice was no more than a whisper.

Johanna nodded. "I got this basket from a seller at the markets. I've known this woman for some time. She is a bit odd and she gets teased a lot, but she can also see things in willow wood. This morning when I saw her, something dreadful, something I think is dark magic, struck her mute—"

"That's because she is an evil practitioner of magic!" He held up the book, as if using it to ward off evil that emanated from Johanna.

"Oh, cowpats!"

His eyes widened. His mouth quivered. He looked like he wanted to say something about language, but couldn't possibly offend the daughter of his boss.

Johanna went on, "The woman gave me the basket. This is the only way she could tell me what happened to her, or what happened at her farm. See, this is how 'evil magic' is used for good, because she can't read or write."

"And, pray, Mistress Johanna, what happened at the farm?"

Johanna had to bite her tongue not to lash out at his pious tone. "That's what I'm not sure about. The wood tells me . . . there are men on horses coming this way. I don't know who they are. Estlander bandits on our borders, perhaps. They have magicians. They have demons. Big, hairy, flat-footed creatures with snarling teeth and strong jaws."

He stiffened, then snorted. "No demons exist. They're a myth perpetuated by the Lord of Fire in order to strike fear into the congregation. The Church of the Triune seeks to exterminate those folk rumours. These are foolish girlish dreams that you're seeing."

And he, of all people, believed this? "Have you ever seen a bear, Master Willems?"

He met her eyes squarely, but said nothing. He hadn't.

"I have." She thought of the sad creature she'd seen in an

Estlander market, chained up to a tree. A bear in its natural state was just a dangerous creature, but those with bear magic could turn it into a demon. That was what the rumours said at least. "I'd be glad to be proven wrong, Master Willems, but what I saw looked very much like demons. I simply wondered if you had seen something similar, because if you have, other people need to know. We should warn the king, or the guards, or whoever will listen. This has nothing to do with dreams. The wood always speaks true. I suspect the wind always speaks true as well. We see the images; it's up to us to ascribe meaning. The basket seller Loesie lives in the Bend, which is where she cut the wood. If the Bend has been invaded, the bandits will be in the marshes and may not be spotted until they're almost in the city. So, I ask again: have you seen anything?"

"No." The denial came too quickly, too defensive. He was sweating and gripping the book with more force than necessary.

"Master Willems, please. There could be trouble on the way."

"The wind does not speak, Mistress Johanna. And you would do well not to mention these things anymore."

"Well then," she said, rising from the chair. "I leave it up to you. I was worried by what I saw, and if you are concerned as well, you don't have to tell me, but do tell someone. Write an unsigned letter, if you are too scared."

"I'm not scared, Mistress Johanna. I will fight this evil magic in all the ways I can."

She left the office more worried than she'd been coming in. And she still had no proof of any trouble that the mayor would believe.

CHAPTER 3

WHEN JOHANNA and Nellie got home, the hallway was filled with the smell of cooking. As they took their coats off in the hall, Koby was just coming up from the kitchen carrying a tray of bowls and terrines.

Johanna followed her into the dining room.

Father already sat at the table. He nodded briefly to her as she sat down.

While Koby ladled soup in their plates, they started their usual talk about business and accounts. Father asked if Pietersen had paid yet, which Johanna informed him he had not, and then he said he'd chase it up. He mentioned that he had heard that Octavio Nieland was interested in buying bigger boats and going into ocean trade. There had been talk of forming a group, because the palace guards were obviously not going to protect the ships, but there would need to be money invested in protection and men and weapons. Anglian ships were in strong competition with the Saarlander ones. They always looked to steal the best trades and more than one skirmish had been fought over trading partners or safe anchorage. Also, there were many strange folk out beyond the Horn. Far Eastern ships with their red, square sails sometimes came all the way to the southern Lurezian coast. They sold silks and spices, but they spoke strange tongues and no one knew much about their rulers or whether they might be hostile.

Father scoffed, tucking his napkin into his collar. "Frankly, I don't understand why the investors tolerate Octavio Nieland, because he upsets everyone with his improper manners. He's too much of a pinchpenny to contribute much to the guards so they're not going to be interested in defending his ships. Have you heard about the time when he accidentally asked a Lurezian duchess to share the bed with him?" He chuckled.

This was Father in his element: ridiculing Octavio Nieland, who was a few years older than Johanna, had recently taken over his ailing father's company and belonged to the noble class that Father so wanted to join but probably never would.

"He meant to say join him on the couch, of course, not the bed. She was most upset, and he did not end up getting the contract that he went to Lurezia to negotiate."

Of course Johanna already knew that through the church gossip. It was amazing what those wooden benches told her, and the story might not be quite as Father told it. The gossip told her that the lady had been flirting, as Lurezians were bound to do.

"My point is, dear daughter, that the boy is not suited to negotiating delicate contracts with foreigners. He will make blunder after blunder and will create a bad name for Saarlander merchants. We could easily step in and show those people that we can be serious about business without offending everyone and making enemies in important places."

Except that Father could not buy any ships outright

because, as a non-noble, he couldn't hire guards. He could only invest his money in other people's ships, and he was too stubborn for that.

"Sea trade will be more important than river trade. I predict that the Far Eastern traders will come into harbour soon enough. We don't want to appear weak—"

That reminded her— "Do you know, by the way, whose dark-coloured sloop is in the harbour? Someone coming to the king's annual ball, I heard."

"I don't follow gossip, you know that, daughter. You might be better off asking your people at church, hmm? All they seem to do is gossip."

Father, please. Koby was still in the room. She went to church. He often said these things just to rile her.

There were voices elsewhere in the house, Nellie letting someone into the front door. A male voice.

"I don't understand why you keep going to that church. That Shepherd is a gibbering idiot. Have you ever heard of such thing as the Triune? A three-headed monster that's supposed to do good on the earth in the name of God. And then they say that they don't believe in magic. Three-headed monsters."

"They are symbols."

"That's not how that dressed-up clown explained it to me—"

"Father!"

"He is a dressed-up clown, and a gibbering idiot, and I'll say so however many times I please in my own house. He was talking real monsters, and believing what he said, too. You know that three-headed monsters can't work? Each head has a mind of its own, and there is no one head to decide which way the monster is going to go if all three want to go in different directions."

He snorted.

Johanna managed to bite her tongue.

A discussion about this was pointless, and they'd had so many of these discussions already. It never got them anywhere.

"Everyone goes to church. People stick out when they don't. People talk about them."

"Octavio Nieland doesn't go."

"He's one of the few. He sticks out, but he doesn't care because he's Octavio Nieland." Also because he belonged to the nobility. He looked down his nose at something like the Church that was born of the common people. The Shepherd was said to have been a poor man, walking from town to town and helping people where he could, and it seemed King Nicholaos understood the commoners better than the nobles did. Johanna disliked many things about the Church, but this wasn't one of them.

"Daughter, you lack the most important ingredient of a believer: belief; and one day that's going to break you up."

He might be right, or he might not. She'd worry about that when the problem came up.

They ate in silence for a while. The big clock against the back wall went tick-tick-tick.

Why did he infuriate her so much lately?

Father put his spoon down and looked at her in a self-important way. "Anyway, daughter, about the ball. It seems I have received an invitation after all. You will be going with me—no, don't look at me like that. It's time that you started behaving a bit more like a lady."

"Father, the ball is in two days' time. I have nothing good enough to wear." If she was to walk up the palace steps under the eyes of all those in Saardam who cared about fashion, even her best shoes wouldn't be good enough, because they were serviceable, not fashionable. Father didn't like to spend a lot of money on clothes, not even hers. She felt the same.

He smiled. "We will have to fix that, then. You'll soon find that you have a visitor coming here who will help you solve that problem."

"You're getting a dress made for me? Now? Don't you want me to do the accounts?"

"Forget about them for these two days." He rose from the table, looking at her with that *you're my little girl* look that he'd used since she was little. "For once, I want you to look your very best. I have to go now. Business calls. I believe my visitor has already arrived."

And he was out the door.

Johanna stared after his back. That had to be the first time that he'd told her to take time off from the accounts. Was there something wrong with him?

When she went into the hall, Father's visitor was already in Father's study, having left behind a scent of tobacco and spice that lingered in the hallway.

She heard a voice in the room. Not Father. Not Captain Pieters of the Brouwer flagship, the *Lady Sara*. Not master de Waard, the manager of the warehouse. Not Jan Hendricksen, one of Father's best customers. Not that annoying Octavio Nieland either, or his elderly father.

An unfamiliar coat hung on the stand. A man's coat. Black. A very finely-made one with a very small pin on the coat's collar: the rooster, the symbol of the Carmine House.

What in all of heaven's name would Father have to say to the royal family?

In the stairwell, on the landing halfway between the ground floor and the second floor, was a little door that led into a low-ceilinged storeroom that had been built between the floors. The servants used this to store items of furniture that they didn't use anymore, or spare plates or tableware that didn't fit in the cupboards. This room was directly above Father's office.

Johanna paused at the stairs, looking carefully if anyone could see her. Then she opened the door quietly, went in and shut it again so that it became dark and stuffy inside. In the little cupboard-like space, she wriggled off her shoes and carried them in her hand while she very slowly climbed up the couple of steps to the room. The steps were odd, at an angle, and uneven. They were made of rough wood that creaked badly unless you were very careful and very slow.

The storeroom was barely tall enough for her to stand in. Father would have to bend his head to avoid hitting it on the ceiling beams. There was a window in the far wall. Half of it vanished below the floor and the bottom part of it was the window in Father's study below. The light that shone through silvered items of furniture covered with sheets and various boxes and crates. One of them had Estlander writing on it. It had belonged to Johanna's mother, Lady Sara Aroden, a minor duchess of the Estlander court.

The sound of father's voice drifted up through the floorboards. Johanna sank to her knees, trying to make not the slightest of sounds, and put her ear to the floor. It was very dusty.

Father was speaking. ". . . We can provide loans, certainly. But I don't know that we have the capacity to do what you ask."

Johanna held her breath. Her nose tickled with the smell of wood that hadn't seen a mop for years.

"I'm not sure I understand your problem. I hear the Brouwer Company is one of the most profitable in all of Saardam." She didn't recognise the voice of this man. He was not the royal family's buyer, who sometimes came to get Estlander cheeses, which was how the Brouwer Company got its royal-approved seal.

Father said again, "That may be as it is, but I still like to invest my money wisely, in a way in which it will see us get returns. I frankly cannot see what this loan is going to do in my favour. And for what, precisely?"

The man from the court coughed, the wet phlegmy cough of a smoker. He said something that Johanna didn't catch, except that it was about the good of the country and something that needed to be defeated.

Johanna's heart thudded. Did the royal family know about these demons crossing the river?

"Drink?" Father said.

Johanna heard him open the door of the cabinet that held the pretty glasses. There was the chink of glass on the metal tray and the glug-glug of brandy being poured.

The silence was uneasy. She hardly dared move, even though her nose was starting to get very itchy and her knees were sore from kneeling on the rough wood.

"You live well, Dirk," the visitor said. "You have all you want—no, don't say anything. I know you want noble status. I know you want it mainly so that you can provide for your daughter by marrying her off well, and that you're waiting for this to happen before she marries."

What?

Father replied, but Johanna didn't hear it because her heart was thudding so loudly.

The man said in reply, "That can be arranged. I will even see to it personally."

"It's starting to sound like blackmail to me. Pay up and you can have what you want."

"No, no, we need people like yourself. We want you to invest in our country."

Father snorted. "The kingdom charges enough taxes to pay for its army. What is wrong with the current size of the army? We're at peace, are we not? Why doesn't the king invest in it, if he thinks it's that important?"

"The king has already invested a considerable amount—"

"In an army?"

"The king looks after the spiritual wellbeing of the people."

"Building churches is investing in the country?"

"The king has made the Church his first priority."

A silence fell. Johanna could just about see Father sit behind his desk swirling his brandy, giving the man a suspicious look. Father was also too smart to voice any of the colourful thoughts he had about the Church.

He said, "Do you have any of the nobility investing in this new army?"

Oh, that question struck home. It said, *Does the nobility still trust the king?* Johanna could almost feel the tension in the room.

The man went on, sounding uneasy. "There have been . . . problems. Not everybody is as lucky as you, Dirk. Many of our merchants have been shunned by buyers across our borders. They don't make anywhere near as much profit as you do."

"It has nothing to do with luck. Before you say any more about luck, you can have all the luck in the world. I would have my wife still around over any luxury I've amassed in my life. I've worked hard at this business and even harder not to offend anyone with ideas. That's why I've done well. I don't play games and I don't judge. And now if you want to get back to our business—"

There was a small squeak from behind Johanna. A shaft of light fell into the room from the hallway.

She turned around and gasped.

"Mistress Johanna!" Nellie stood at the bottom of the steps, her mouth open in shock. "You're eavesdropping on your father? That's terrible!"

"Shhhh!" Johanna rose and tiptoed out the room back into

the stairwell and shut the door behind her. On the stairs, she slipped her feet back into her shoes.

"Mistress, aren't you too old for this sort of behaviour? It's bad enough for children, but a lady your age should definitely know better—"

"Father's got a visitor from the court. They're talking about . . ." But she wasn't sure if she should tell Nellie what they were talking about. If what she heard was right, and she understood it correctly, the palace was in financial trouble and the nobles didn't want to support the king, and the king thought that a threat to the country was strong enough to warrant a bigger army.

She shivered, seeing men on horseback and demons. Did this mean that the king knew about the demons?

Nellie said, "Anyway, I came to look for you because you have a visitor."

CHAPTER 4

NELLIE PRECEDED Johanna into the formal room to the right of the main entrance. The door was opposite Father's study, whose door was still closed. A smell of smoke seeped into the hall. She also smelled perfume that definitely didn't come from Father's visitor.

Johanna went into the formal room and found that her visitor was Mistress Daphne, the Lurezian seamstress. She waited, primly seated on a chair next to the hearth. She was perhaps ten years older than Johanna, tall and elegant, a dark-haired southern beauty. Today she wore a plain working dress in moss green with little edges of lace at the sleeves. She might not look spectacular, but as far as fashion went, she was the best of the best. She knew how to dress to look elegant and not take any attention away from her well-heeled clientele.

"Good afternoon, Mistress Johanna." She rose and bowed.

Her face was prim and stiff, but Johanna didn't miss the faint twinge of disapproval and her glance at Johanna's house shoes and plain dress. Johanna cringed. In the eyes of this woman, she was as a dirty riverboat to the owner of a large seafaring ship. That was her life: plain, serviceable, sensible.

"I am here to arrange your dress," Mistress Daphne said. "Your father wants me to supply you with a dress that will make you look like a princess, so he said. I heard that he was so lucky as to get a last-moment invite to the ball at the palace tomorrow night." Mistress Daphne said all this with a prim face, as though she clearly despaired at the prospect of making Johanna presentable. "I told him that it would be impossible to have a gown made, but I always have a couple of sample gowns that I can adapt, so you may yet be in luck." Mistress Daphne picked up a pile of boxes she had brought. "You have little enough time to choose, so we better get started now."

Johanna glanced at the strange curly writing on the side of the boxes. She was pretty sure, from the lessons Father had made her take, that it was Lurezian. Each box was a work of art in itself, made from fine board, with carefully painted patterns and held closed with a coloured ribbon.

Mistress Daphne picked up the first box, set it down on the couch, pulled the ribbon and took off the lid. Inside lay a shimmering dress in vivid blue, all lace, frills and ruffles. Johanna saw noble girls walk the streets in dresses like this sometimes—that airhead Julianna Nieland for example—and thought they looked like sugar cakes.

Mistress Daphne held it up.

"Oh, it's so beautiful!" Nellie said. "Try it on, Mistress Johanna."

That thing? She'd look like a dressed-up troll. Frills and ruffles were for shapely girls, but courtesy of her mother's Estlander blood, Johanna was tall for a girl and didn't have much shape, unless you counted "barge pole" as a shape.

"I'm not sure about the colour," she said, eying the other boxes and hoping they contained something less frilly.

"Blue is all the fashion this year," Mistress Daphne said, running an experienced and critical eye over Johanna's long legs. "If you would just try it on, I can guarantee you will look stunning in this dress. This is a very special one I had shipped straight from Lurezia. It's from the modistes of the House of Giron, their latest design collection."

It meant nothing to Johanna, and worse, she couldn't get excited about it. She pretended to look interested, but just couldn't pretend any longer. "Can I see the other ones?"

Mistress Daphne seemed disappointed, but did open the other three boxes she had brought: two of the dresses were frillier than the blue one, and one of them was even pink. The third one was a dark red, rather plain number. Plain and simple, like her.

"I like that one the best," Johanna said.

"Well then, let's try it on."

Mistress Daphne laid the dress out while Johanna took off her overclothes, placing her house shoes discretely behind the couch, and hoping no one would say anything about them.

Mistress Daphne came to help her into the dress, doing up the countless fiddly little buttons on the back.

"This itches," Johanna said. "And it's too loose."

"I know. We can fix that." Mistress Daphne took a box of pins and started pinning the sides of the bodice together.

"You look so pretty," Nellie said.

Johanna snorted, standing there with her arms spread. She didn't *want* to look pretty. All those noble girls would only gawk at her. She understood that Father wanted to go to the ball because there would be foreign people to talk business, and of course he couldn't go alone, and he had no handy widow friends to accompany him, so she would have to do. But it would be terrible, and boring. And no one would want to talk to her.

"There are rumours Prince Roald is to attend the ball," Mistress Daphne said at her back.

"Is he really?" Nellie said.

"That's the rumour. There was a Burovian ship in port this morning that's said to have brought him, but it arrived late last night and no one saw the passengers disembark."

"I saw that ship." Johanna remembered the sloop she'd seen in the harbour, the sleek one with the cabin and the red curtains.

Prince Roald, really?

"It looks like the King is trying to keep it a surprise," Mistress Daphne said, in a conspiratorial tone. "I've heard it said that, last night, the Shepherd even locked the church doors when the royal family came in for prayer, so that no one would see the prince."

Johanna wondered where Mistress Daphne got that information. Did she see things in willow wood, too? Surely Johanna could have told if that was the case. The gift of magic wasn't common in Lurezian people anyway.

Nellie's eyes were wide. "Does that mean Prince Roald is cured?"

"That depends on what's wrong with him," Johanna said. There were rumours about that, too. That the king didn't control his son's tempers and had sent him away so that he could be disciplined and taught manners by monks, or that the prince had some incurable illness.

"Sickly children will often end up growing into healthy adults," Mistress Daphne said primly. "Given plenty of food and fresh air."

Whatever she knew about it, not having children herself. "Roald is past childhood." Johanna was born in what was termed "the prince's year" and she was reminded often enough that she was fast getting too old to be married. Roald was a month older than she was.

"Maybe the king has decided that Roald is well enough to take his position as crown prince," Nellie said.

"It's not as if he's got another option. With Celine—"

"Mistress Johanna, why do you always have to think the worst of people?"

Johanna turned around to face Nellie. "I don't, providing those people do their job. If King Nicholaos chose to make his second child his heir, then there must have been a reason for it. If he chose to send Roald away, even after Celine's death, there must be something going on. Roald is his only remaining child. Why hasn't he been at the palace learning how to rule the country? There has to be a reason. And I'm not sure if I like it. If Roald was too ill to learn, then why hasn't one of the King's cousins come to take Celine's place? That's all I want to know."

"Stand still," Mistress Daphne admonished, her mouth full of pins.

Nellie blushed. "You mustn't speak of the king like that, Mistress Johanna."

"Tell me then what else I should think. I'm worried. The royal family is small. If Roald can't do the job, then one of his cousins should. King Nicholaos is not getting any younger." Or, for that matter, any saner. Rumours about how much money he gave to the Church were hard to miss. And the conversation she had overheard in her father's room only added to her worry.

Neither Nellie nor Mistress Daphne dared venture a further opinion. They all knew why none of the other royals had helped out. None of Roald's cousins lived in Saardam and Johanna was sure any of his cousins would be deeply unpopular with the genteel folk of Saardam.

Bah, nobles.

Mistress Daphne finished pinning up the dress and stepped back, looking Johanna up and down.

Johanna cringed. She hated it when people judged her looks, and those dresses made her resemble a dressed-up garden rake.

Mistress Daphne wheeled the mirror across the room, that one where Johanna could almost see her little finger-prints on the glass and hear her mother say, "Don't touch," in her Estlander accent. She'd been four or five then.

The young woman that looked back at her in the mirror didn't seem familiar. The dark dress made her look stern, and the parts where Mistress Daphne had taken in the sides the skirt didn't sit properly. She tugged at it.

"That will be fixed," Mistress Daphne said. Judging by the small shake of her head, she didn't seem to like the result.

To be honest, Johanna didn't like it either. The sleeves were long and tight, the neckline was high, and the dark red made her look very old.

She admitted defeat. "I guess I should try a different dress?"

Mistress Daphne sighed a little happy sigh. "Your exuber-ance does not deserve something so . . . dour. You are not a matron; you're a maiden."

"Did I mention I don't like wearing frilly dresses?"

"You are truly different from the other girls, Mistress Johanna." Johanna didn't know if that was meant as an insult or a compliment. Probably both. "Given approval by their fathers, the other girls would choose the frilliest, the finest dresses I have. Will you just humour me and try on the blue one?"

"Yes, try it," Nellie said.

Johanna eyed the box, still open, on the table. Horrible. Frilly. Like a sugar cake.

She didn't want to go to the ball. She hated pomp. But going to the ball was obviously important for Father. She let out a frustrated breath. "All right."

Mistress Daphne undid all the fiddly buttons and helped her out of the red dress into the blue one. The colour was exquisite; she had to hand it to the weavers and their experimenting with exotic ingredients. The fabric was a material that looked to her like silk, but Mistress Daphne said it was something called taffeta, a material that was much stiffer than silk and allowed the puffed-up sleeves to stay puffed up by themselves. The bodice was embroidered with tiny beads and silver thread.

"Hold your hands up, Mistress Johanna."

Johanna did and Mistress Daphne tightened the lace at the back. The bodice drew tight around her waist.

"Does it have to be so tight?" She put her hand on her side. Her hand met taut and stiff fabric threaded with whalebone straps to keep it in place. The top of the corset squeezed her breasts so that they were pushed together in a way they normally weren't. And very *visible*. Johanna put her hand on the bare skin of her chest.

"I modified the dress. The Lurezian version has a much lower neckline, showing more skin, but the palace wouldn't approve of that at all."

"Even more skin?" Johanna could see right down into the slit between her pale breasts where sunlight never came and where her skin was free of freckles.

"Yes, sometimes you can even see the indecent parts—who are you taking to the ball, Mistress Johanna?"

"I presume I'm only there so Father doesn't have to go alone."

"Pfaw, don't be silly," Mistress Daphne said around the pins in her mouth. "You should look at every young man there. You are not getting any younger."

Except they would all be nobles and would look down on her, not to mention insufferable bores who could only talk of the latest spoils of hunting expeditions. Johanna would be required to talk to the even more boring women, who only cared about who wore what.

Mistress Daphne stepped back. "Now, how is that, Mistress Johanna? Of course, you will have to do your hair, and add jewellery."

Nellie looked dubious. "It does show a lot of skin."

Mistress Daphne dragged the dressing mirror across the floor. Johanna had been right: This dress did make her look like a sugar cake. She pulled at the frills on her shoulders, secretly wishing they'd all come off.

Mistress Daphne nodded. "Don't you think that looks much better?"

Johanna turned around in front of the mirror. Frills everywhere, even on her back. It was horrible. But she had to admit that this dress fitted better. And in a rebellious way, she liked the low neckline. The bold colour made her eyes come out. The dress was a bit rebellious against everything. A bit like wearing clogs to church. The Shepherd told the flock in church that women had to cover up and be modest. The same Shepherd who said that all magic was evil.

"Don't you think it looks gorgeous on her?" Mistress Daphne said.

Nellie nodded. "You look like a princess, just like your father wanted."

"You think so?" Johanna looked at Mistress Daphne.

Some part of her still hoped that either of them would say that she couldn't possibly wear this in public.

They didn't.

Mistress Daphne nodded appreciatively. "It looks very good. Julianna Nieland tried it on, but she was too short to wear it."

And with that, she sold it. Johanna would do anything to annoy Julianna Nieland.

CHAPTER 5

MISTRESS DAPHNE packed the other dresses away, and then got into taking serious measurements. Johanna stood barefooted, with her hands spread wide, while Mistress Daphne put pins on every panel of the dress, until Johanna wondered if there would be anything left of the original design when she finished. Mistress Daphne and Nellie talked about fashion and fabrics, and Johanna was keen to be let out of the pincushion prison.

There was the sound of voices in the hall, and then at the door. Father's visitor was leaving, and it frustrated her that she still had no idea who he was. A bit later, she heard the distinctive tread of Koby coming up the stairs, and then the sound of the tableware cupboard being opened and plates being put on the table. She'd been locked up in this room talking *clothes* all afternoon.

"I think dinner is ready," she said. She wanted to be out of that dress. She needed to go to see Loesie as she promised. Loesie would want to know what Johanna had done about her warning, and she couldn't tell her any good news. *I spent all afternoon being measured for a dress,* or *No one would believe me,* wouldn't be statements Loesie understood. People from the land never questioned wind magic and willow magic. That was also why Johanna liked Loesie: because she didn't have to explain her magic or apologise for it.

"It's done," Mistress Daphne said, and she started unlacing the back of the dress until Johanna could step out. "I'll work on this, and have it ready for you tomorrow night."

After stiff fabric and all those pins, Johanna's old clothes felt like a comfortable blanket. She felt like she never wanted to take them off again, never mind what people said about them.

She left Nellie and Mistress Daphne to their gossip and went into the hall.

The smell of tobacco and spice still lingered in the air. The door to Father's study was open, but there was no one inside the room. The black coat with the Carmine House pin was gone from the coat stand. A fire burned low in the hearth and the scent of brandy and tobacco lingered.

They called this the Green Room. On one side, there was a table surrounded by chairs with silk cushions. The entire left-hand wall was taken up by a glass-fronted cupboard with shelves full of books. Most of those were Johanna's, bought for her by Father on his travels. Above the hearth hung a portrait of Johanna's grandfather.

Father himself sat at the table in the dining room, while Koby ladled soup in a gold-rimmed soup plate.

Johanna took her place opposite him and Koby came to fill her plate, too. Leek soup. It smelled heavenly. "Thanks, Koby."

Koby nodded and walked out, leaving behind a woolly sort of silence that stretched while they both ate. He had changed into the comfortable woollen vest which his sister Aunt Dianne had knitted for him. His short beard was now more grey than blond, and the hair that he so carefully combed over his bald spots hung down his neck in a greying ponytail.

"You sorted yourself out with a dress?" he asked. "I presume you've seen Mistress Daphne?" So, he wasn't going to tell her who the mystery visitor had been.

"I have."

"Has she made sure you got something pretty?" The wrinkles around his eyes crinkled with a brief smile.

Johanna shrugged. She wanted to show her displeasure over his avoiding the subject of the visitor, but he would probably get angry with her. "I got a dress."

"What colour?"

"Blue." The dress would probably turn a few heads, even if only Julianna Nieland's.

"I trust she'll have you looking like a real lady."

"Don't you start, too, Father."

"It's becoming more important that you take life a bit more seriously, young lady."

Something about that remark made Johanna shiver. He wasn't going to talk about this getting married thing, was he? "How did you get an invite to go to the palace?"

"It was a stroke of luck," he said, thoughtfully spooning soup out of his plate. "Mind you, I'm not going for fun. Most of the ball will be to conduct business."

"Did you apply to the council of nobles again?"

He put his spoon down, and seemed to deliberately avoid her eyes. Eventually, he said, "No. As long as the old Nieland is alive, there's probably little point in trying that avenue again. But, there may be another way."

"Another way into the nobility?"

Koby came in with a tray that contained gold-rimmed platters with carved duck and mash gravy, and another platter with sliced bread. Father said nothing while she set the things out on the table.

He spoke again only after she left. "This is not common knowledge, so I prefer you told no one about this—"

"Do I ever gossip about things you tell me?" He infuriated her so much. The twists and turns he took, the avoidance, the right angles in his conversation. Why couldn't he just talk straight?

He sighed. "Prince Roald is back, and will be confirmed as the king's successor at the ball tomorrow night."

"Tell me something new. He came on that Burovian ship that's still in the harbour, didn't he?"

Father smiled briefly. "I should have known that you were smart enough to figure it out."

"Is he cured?"

He flicked his eyebrows and continued eating his soup, in that infuriating way he would go silent when she most wanted him to speak.

The old clock on the wall went tick-tick-tick. Next to it hung a portrait of an elegant brown-haired woman. She wore a beautiful green dress—buttoned up to the neck—and a string of pearls. Lady Sara Aroden, Johanna's mother. How would she have coped with Father's infuriating silences?

Eventually he said, "Prince Roald will assume his duties as of tomorrow night." As if she had asked nothing.

"What was wrong with him? Why has he been away for so long?"

Father held up his hands. "Johanna, none of this is meant to be public knowledge. There will be royal announcements about this at the ball, and you will be there to hear it from the king's mouth."

She restrained a snort. As if the king would tell the good nobles all the details about his family. If he hadn't done so when they first decided to make Celine the crown princess, he certainly wouldn't do so now.

"Why were we invited?" Mother and Father had been to

these balls at time, but usually that was because of some business thing, like that time when Father had opened up trade with the lands beyond Estland and some of those people happened to be guests at the palace.

Father gave a half-smile. "The Brouwer family seems to be going places, after all." He put his spoon down.

Johanna sensed the importance of his words. "Is this about the visitor you just had? He was from the royal family, wasn't he?" Just what was Father getting into? *There were other ways?*

Other ways of what? Was he buying his way into the nobility?

Wait.

The crown prince was back to resume his duties. The prince was twenty-four. His duties would include finding a wife and getting busy with producing an heir.

She and Father looked at each other and she saw in his eyes that he knew what she was thinking.

He nodded, slowly. "King Nicholaos has issued a call for all ladies of good standing to attend the ball for a dance with the prince."

Johanna opened her mouth—

"No, Johanna. Do your old father a pleasure and for once do as I say. The king has fallen out badly with most of the city's nobles. Many of those so-called nobles don't even have half the capital that we do. You are the most eligible lady from the new merchant class."

"You have got to be kidding! I thought you wanted me to look after the company."

"I do."

"How could I do that if I'm choking in ruffles and court ladies?" And she'd just asked Mistress Daphne for that ridiculously frilly dress.

"My guess is: better than if you marry Octavio Nieland."

"But . . ." Johanna stopped there. "Octavio Nieland?"

"Yes. He's been in my office several times to ask for your hand in marriage."

"But why? The Nielands hate us!"

"They only hate what they can't get. The best way to stifle a competitor who frightens you is by marrying into their family."

"But . . ." The Nielands were nobles. The very ones who scorned Father. Why did he involve himself with them?

"Johanna. He's very insistent. You amuse him, he says. He wants a strong woman who is able to look after his affairs when he goes to sea. I'm not going to be able to say no to him indefinitely. Not if there is no other option."

No other option?

She had assumed that he had been happy enough not to let her marry. Not Octavio Nieland, not anyone. She'd just continue to do the work he'd been doing, without the need for a man. She'd shown him that she could do it.

One thing she hadn't considered: he saw her marrying to the advantage of the company. Tears of anger sprang to her eyes.

"I thought you loved me," she said, her voice unsteady.

"I do love you, and that's why I'm trying to get you the best I can negotiate. The prince desperately needs to marry. At the ball tomorrow night he will be presented with Saardam's most eligible ladies. I've negotiated one dance for you with him. The court adviser who was just here has let me know that the king looks favourably upon you. Take the opportunity to present yourself well and he may want to see you again. It seems fortunate, perhaps, that King Nicholaos has made a lot of enemies amongst the nobles with his insistence on church donations. We are successful, and the royal family wants support from successful traders, and they desperately need an heir from a family that goes to church. We can provide those things."

He thought of the rest of her life like that? Something to be bartered?

Johanna rose from the table, throwing her spoon down. "I'm not hungry anymore."

"It upsets you."

"Of course it upsets me." She tried very hard to keep the anger out of her voice, but didn't succeed entirely. "How can you just drop this on me like that?"

"Just one dance, Johanna."

"And what if he likes me . . . or what if he doesn't? Would you honestly expect me to marry Octavio Nieland after all the bad things you said about him?"

"I don't want you to, no. But if you don't marry and I die, our wealth goes to my useless cousin. I want that even less than I want the company to go to the Nielands."

"Do I get a say in this?"

"I've waited years for you to have a say. You don't look like making up your mind any time soon."

"I don't want to get married. Look at the girls who used to be my friends. Claire got married. I never see her anymore. Does she even leave the house? Augustina got married, and her husband won't even let her do any shopping. Willemina got married and she's got so many children that she has no time for anything else. They never go out. They rarely talk to me anymore. Does that look like fun?"

He slammed his flat palm on the table. "This is not about fun!"

The explosion of his voice shocked her into silence.

He took a deep breath, nostrils flaring and went on, "You are behaving like a spoilt child. I'm thinking I've waited far too long already. There is a lot more to marriage than two people. It's about their families and their combined wealth and business."

"*You* married for love." Not only that, her mother's parents had let their daughter go off with a foreigner.

"I was extremely lucky."

Johanna, on the other hand, was in danger of becoming an old spinster, and at this point in time, she was just a piece of property to be moved around for maximum gain.

She got that message loud and clear.

"I won't be around forever, and I worry about what would happen to you if you don't have a family—no, don't tell me that you're happy to run the company by yourself. I know you are, and I know you're capable, but things don't work that way in this world, do they? No one will do business with a woman who runs the company by herself. And it's getting worse because of that stupid Church."

Johanna looked down, tears pricking in her eyes. She knew, and had always known. The world was changing. It had no room for happily unmarried women.

"Please, Johanna. One dance with him. Chat to him. Try your best. Because I wouldn't give my company to Octavio Nieland over my dead body."

After one long stare, Johanna left the room without speaking.

CHAPTER 6

IN THE SUMMER the nights were long, and after that disastrous evening meal, Johanna slipped down the stairs into the servants' quarters. The house staff, Koby, Nellie, the gardener, all sat around the kitchen table. The sounds of spoons clinking against plates drifted from the room, as well as talk and laughter. Johanna always felt a bit jealous hearing them chat and laugh. She wished she could join them and laugh with them instead of having to suffer Father's long silences.

She slipped into the pantry and grabbed a half-cut loaf of bread and a piece of soft cheese, which she put in a basket.

Then she went out the back door into the garden with its pebbles and neatly-clipped bushes. The roses were very prolific this year and the scent of the flowers hung heavy in the summer air.

Johanna walked past the garden house—where her grand-parents from Aroden used to stay when they visited, but that was now full of old furniture—and out the back gate into the street.

Passers-by greeted her, but she was too absorbed in her angry thoughts to take much notice of them.

Prince Roald!

What was her father thinking? As if anyone would take her seriously when she came to dance with the prince. All the noble girls would laugh, and the prince would know her for what she was the moment she opened her mouth.

Even if the prince was the most dashing, romantic young man, it would not work. Princes did not marry merchant daughters.

She was more concerned about what Father had said about Octavio Nieland. Octavio was the biggest piece of arrogance in the Saardam gentry. When he set his sights on something, he usually got it, in his unforgiving and blunt way. She did *not* want to marry Octavio Nieland.

The harbour was quiet at this time of day, with the boats dark and locked up. All the ships' boys had gone home, the wind had calmed and the only sound that disturbed the silence was the slap of waves against ship hulls and the creaking of planks or boards.

The Brouwer Company's sea cow barn was at the end of the quay, behind a couple of warehouses and behind where the boys had moored the *Lady Sara* now that the hold was empty.

Johanna walked past the large warehouse doors where her footsteps sounded loud. A cat stalked along the wharf, waving the tip of its tail. A couple of deck hands were still talking somewhere. She could hear their voices although she couldn't see them, the sound echoing weirdly here.

The dark Burovian sloop that had brought Prince Roald from wherever he had been still lay moored at the quay, giving up none of its secrets. Prince Roald? Really?

Johanna didn't remember him very well, because even before he left, he rarely came outside. Part of her hoped that he'd come back healthy, as a handsome young man who would fall in love the moment he saw her. Yeah, like that was going to happen. Like she even wanted it to happen.

She opened the door to Father's barn and stepped into its inky darkness. Something rustled in the corner.

"Loesie?"

"Hmmmm."

Johanna turned up the wick on the oil lamp that always burned in the corner. By its measly light, a sea cow rose to the surface of the water and cast a baleful look at her. Its eye, brown and mournful, looked surprisingly human. The surface of the water looked oily, with a mess of cabbage leaves floating around. Ripples disturbed the surface where the other cows were. Also, occasionally there would be a trail of bubbles escaping from the animals' pelts or other places.

On the right-hand wall the harnesses hung on hooks, with thick oiled leather straps that held the pack to the front of the boat on the upriver runs. Underneath the harnesses was a workbench and tools for repair.

Johanna put the basket on the bench.

"I've got bread and cheese for you."

Loesie came out of the darkness. In that horrible black dress and her translucent pale skin and eyes so wide that the whites showed on all sides, she looked like a wraith.

She snatched the bread and held it to her chest like a trea-sure needing protection. She shuffled aside, like a mangy dog afraid to be hit.

"Loesie?" A chill went over Johanna's back. She was no longer sure that it had been a good idea to come here alone.

"Ghghghghghg!" Loesie darted forwards and grabbed the basket. She snatched the cheese and bit into it.

While she chewed, she put her hands on the handle of the basket. She closed her eyes and let the magic of the wood flow through her. She opened her mouth and uttered a soft cry. A pale white dribble of half-chewed cheese ran down her chin.

"Loesie, what's wrong?" The chill that Johanna had felt earlier grew into a blizzard.

What sort of dark craft did it take to put a spell this strong on a person? What else had been affected other than Loesie's ability to speak? How could she know that Loesie wasn't leading her into a horrible trap? She'd heard the stories of people turning other people into diseased ghosts. The stories about madmen who devoured blood or human flesh *were* stories, weren't they?

Loesie's eyes opened as slits of pure white. She tilted her head to the ceiling of the barn and swayed from one foot to the other while uttering a low moan.

Johanna backed away.

No, definitely not a good idea to come here.

Loesie came towards her, holding out the basket. "Ghghghghghghgh!"

She tried to push the basket into Johanna's hands, but Johanna wanted nothing to do with it anymore.

"Keep away from me!" Johanna's back bumped into the barn door. She lifted the bar, pushed the door open and ran.

Johanna ran down the wharf, past the dark shadows of boats. Her footsteps sounded loud on the cobbled ground. The cat she'd seen earlier gave a surprised meow and skittered out of her way, into the open door of a warehouse.

There was a light within and a few deck hands were inside, moving barrels. The warehouse belonged to an Estlander merchant but long-time citizen of Saardam, Master Deim. Those Estlanders had odd customs, still working after dark. They must have received an important shipment.

Johanna didn't want the men to see her, because they'd ask what she was doing here. They'd see that she was upset. They would discover Loesie and the state she was in. They might even tell the mayor, or the king's guard, and instead of going to the ball, Johanna would be spending tomorrow night locked up in a cell. No one still did witch burnings anymore, did they?

She ran past the entrance when the men's backs were turned. She ran past the other warehouses and the forbidding walls of the King's guard armoury, where the single guard on duty followed her with his eyes.

She stopped in front of her father's office, catching her breath. The windows were dark. Of course Master Willems had gone home long ago. He was the only one she could talk to about magic, and even he avoided the subject. She couldn't go and see him at home, because his father would be there, and he was with the Church. Visiting him at home would be inappropriate.

Then what?

Panting, she looked back over the wharf, past the warehouses, the ammunition depot and the barn and the *Lady Sara*. There was no movement on the wharf.

Johanna wiped her face, seeing Loesie's wild expression when she closed her eyes, that dribble of half-chewed cheese down her chin.

Had she been wrong to shelter someone who was clearly possessed by evil? And was Loesie now trying to make her a victim as well? Was Master Willems right in saying that nothing had happened upriver? Could Loesie possibly have imbued the wood with the images for the evil purpose of seducing Johanna into the influence of evil?

She shivered.

Loesie, as Johanna remembered her, was a kind young woman. Yes, she was a bit odd, and loved scaring people with her strange tales of creatures that came out of the river next to her grandpa's farm, most of which were stories she made up.

Loesie loved playing pranks. She'd tell an outrageous story and see how far in she could get before her audience understood that she was telling them fibs.

But this . . .

Looks like reality caught up with the prankster.

White eyes, a dribble of milk-like fluid from her mouth—that was how scholars identified people who were possessed by demons.

Her little voice of sanity said, *It was only half-eaten cheese.*

But what about Loesie's eyes? They had definitely turned all-white, without irises.

Johanna wanted to run home and forget that all this had happened. She wanted to burn the basket that Loesie had given her and that sat on the chair by the window in her room.

Then again, Loesie was always a bit strange, but kind-hearted. Loesie would never harm anyone.

A little voice inside her said, *If Loesie had turned into a demon, then the evil would have taken complete possession of her and would not have taken only her voice, right?*

Coming from a farm, Loesie wouldn't read or write. Her voice was the only way in which she could warn people.

The question remained: how much of the real Loesie was still in there?

What to do, what to do?

Whatever happened, she couldn't abandon a friend, because no one else would help her, but she couldn't handle this alone either.

Johanna had started walking again. She came past the harbour-side bars where the sound of yelling male voices spilled out. Through the windows, she could see patrons sitting around tables served by the young man who was the son of the owner. A single dark-haired woman sat on one of the tables. Johanna knew her, too.

Helena had come to Saardam as First Mate's pet aboard one of the southern sea's vessels. After two months at sea, her belly started swelling. She drank a concoction that was supposed to rid her of the child, but it had made her so ill that the First Mate ditched her as soon as they came into port. Helena managed the rooms upstairs, where a never-ending line of sailors were keen to part with their hard-earned money to spend some time with any of the young women Helena had plucked off the streets in towns along the Saar River. She also knew which men were out of work and was a good contact for hiring deck hands.

Johanna crossed the markets where the trestle tables had been packed away until the next market day. On the far side, the belltower of the church reached for the heavens, like a dark shadow against the sky. A light was on in the porch, flickering with the breeze. Hadn't the Shepherd Romulus said that the church doors were always open?

Johanna hesitated, looking around. Apart from the church, the other main building at the markets was the market house. During the day, its front and side doors were open, and merchants would bring in their wares to be officially weighed by market officials. At night, the doors were closed. Few private houses surrounded the markets, and in those that did, the curtains were closed over the windows. Something rustled in the shadows that might be a mouse or a rat, or one of the cats employed to catch those pests. There were no people in sight.

Quietly, Johanna walked up the church steps into the darkness of the porch, into the glow of the flapping flame of the storm light that hung on the back wall of the porch, and pushed the door open. It creaked.

It was not completely dark in the church either. Oil lamps set in sconces on pillars that supported the roof spread an orange glow just strong enough for her to see the aisle. Candles burned at the altar.

Her footsteps sounded hollow in the large space and for once she was glad that she wasn't wearing her clogs.

The church was a reflective space, with simple glass windows, plain pillars and plain wooden pews. The only thing that had any prominence inside the building was a large statue at the front. The three-headed demon stood on its hind legs, with its front legs slightly in the air. It had the body of a strong dog, with muscular legs and shoulders. The three heads were those of an emaciated ghost, a dog and a man. Father was right: it was a hideous thing, but it was meant to be: it symbolised the ugliness of human emotions the Church sought to change.

There were footsteps at the back of the church and a man in a simple robe dissolved from the shadows. Shepherd Romulus.

"Can I help you, child?"

"I . . . um . . ." There was no going back now.

He came towards her in the aisle. From close up, under the candlelight, he looked older than he did in the service. He wore his customary brown robe, a simple garment without any embellishments except the white knotted cord around his waist. He had grey hair cropped short and a short beard, also grey. His green eyes were kind, but surrounded by a spider's web of wrinkles.

"You look disturbed, child."

You would, too, if you'd seen a person possessed by evil. But she said only, "I came here to pray."

He smiled. "You're in the right place for that. Do you want to pray together?"

That seemed like a good starting point. Better than the question she would have to ask later: *What can I do to exorcise a demon from my friend?* Because that question would mean acknowledging that magic existed, or maybe even that she had magic.

Johanna sat next to the Shepherd in the front pew, directly opposite the giant statue of the three-headed Triune. The light cast deep shadows over the dog face that jutted out above her. An angry and snarling thing it was, depicting the evil Spirit in the Triune. The head of the Ghost was on the far side of the statue, a long-haired man with hollow eyes, and the middle head embodied the Holy God, a man with a kind face and a short beard. He looked a bit like King Nicholaos, although she'd seen children clipped on the ear for saying that.

The Reverend folded his hands in his lap and neither of them said anything for a while. The calm beauty of the place soothed Johanna's rattled mind. The wood under her hands showed images of people filing into the church and taking place in the pews. See? There was nothing to panic about. There might be demons and bandits on horseback in the border regions. They might even be on their way to Saardam. But the city was strong and the king's guards would deal with them. She ordered her thoughts into a couple of perfectly rational questions.

"I seek advice about a friend," she said when the Shepherd raised his head.

"Is this a friend who has strayed off the right path?"

"A friend who is possessed." Did she see him do a little double take? "She has lost her voice and her sanity, and speaks gibberish. Maybe she's trying to tell me something, but I can't understand her."

He gave her a thoughtful and calculating look. "Does she roll her eyes and secrete fluids?"

Johanna nodded, and the chill of seeing the white slits of Loesie's eyes returned.

His expression went hard. "She is possessed by evil. Any such should be banished from the city."

"She's my friend. She frightens me, but I have to look after her or no one else will. I don't think she has anyone left in the world. I know her as a kind person, and this is not her fault. Please tell me how to help her."

He turned around and fixed her with his green eyes. "Your heart is kind, sister, but playing with evil will beget more evil. You can pray for her, but the evil of magic is strong. You should not get further involved with her."

"Should I let her die then? She can't look after herself like this." It was a wonder that Loesie had even made it to the markets.

"Your friend is already dead. All that's inside her is the spirit of evil." He folded his hands before his chest as if in prayer.

"She tries to talk to me. She recognises me."

The Shepherd put a hand on her shoulder. "Sister, I see that this upsets you. But demons take on the memories of human bodies. They seek to seduce us with something we want, maybe the voice of someone long ago deceased. Take it from me: most likely, this demon has killed your friend already."

Johanna again heard the penetrating woman's scream that Loesie's basket had played back to her. She didn't *think* it was Loesie's voice, but from that sound, it was hard to tell.

"If, however, your friend's soul is still alive, the demon will leave after it has completed its task. For that reason alone, it is better not to stay close to her."

"You're sure?" How could he know all this? "Have you seen this happen?"

"It's written in the Book." He reached in the pocket of his robe and drew out a well-thumbed copy of the Book of the

Triune. With a pale-fingered hand he leafed through the pages. His fingers trembled.

"Ah, here it is." He pressed the book open and read. "Two days after the encounter on the road, Coran woke up one morning, speaking in tongues. No one in his household, not even his dear wife, could understand what he said. They were afraid and went into the church for guidance, but the Shepherd was not there, since he had gotten up at dawn to spread wards around the edges of the village. When they returned home, Coran was gone as well, and the villagers reported seeing him wander around the fields that surrounded the village for days. Although he had no weapon, his hands were covered in blood. He would not reply if they spoke to him, and would not look them in the eye. His eyes were rolling in his head and when he tried to speak, milk-like fluid would leak from his mouth. After four days, the madness vanished from his eyes, and he came back home, clean and washed. When his family asked him about his absence, he said that he had seen much evil and would never speak to a demon ever again. The next day, the neighbour who had been cheating found his prize cow dead in the paddock, ripped to shreds."

Johanna knew that passage. It was a metaphor for a man learning his lesson after trying to make financial gains at the expense of his neighbour. It held no authority on the subject of demons.

She clenched her hands in her lap, biting her tongue in frustration. There was so much she wanted to say about magic, that it wasn't always evil, that it belonged to objects and not people, that some people couldn't help being able to see it. That you were born with it and it was not something you could choose to engage in, or, for that matter, disengage from. But this was probably not the right time.

"Who is this friend of yours, pray?"

"Someone I know from the markets." She also couldn't say

why she knew Loesie—because they both had willow magic, because she had felt the magic in Loesie that first day she'd met her at the markets as a little girl. "She comes in from the eastern border. She's seen evil things that are coming this way. She may be possessed, but her mind is still fighting the demon. I don't believe that she's evil. And I don't believe that the demon has taken her over completely. I want to know how we can get rid of the demon and restore her speech."

The Shepherd's face became a closed mask. "You're asking for someone who can perform an exorcism. The Church does not provide these people. Exorcisms are quackery that most likely make matters worse than they are. Demons are manifestations of the Triune. They are repelled by prayer, not by fake magicians with horseshoes, goat's blood and other items that wouldn't look out of place in the Lord of Fire's dungeons."

Johanna had never seen an exorcism and had no idea how it was done or if it was effective, but she didn't believe him anymore. He didn't care about Loesie.

What was more, she suddenly had an irrational desire to get out of there. This church was not a place where she could get answers. This Triune was not her friend.

CHAPTER 7

JOHANNA SPENT most of the night worrying about Loesie and what to do. She could only try to imagine how scared her friend must feel, and this made her more determined to ignore the Shepherd's advice to stay away from her. She couldn't leave Loesie to her own devices, *especially* not now.

When Johanna came into the barn the next morning with breakfast, she found Loesie sitting on the side of the walkway, dangling her legs over the water. For a moment, it looked like she had been cured, but when she turned around, her eyes were still wide. She looked so thin and sickly.

Johanna knelt and put down the basket with food at a safe distance, never losing sight of Loesie. "I've brought you eggs and bread, a piece of ham, some butter and cheese."

Loesie dragged the basket over.

"Do you need any more help? I can get you onto the river barge so you can go back home."

"Ghghghghghgh!" Loesie shook her head.

"You don't want to go home?"

"Ghghghghghgh!" More headshaking.

"You can't go home? Where is your family?"

"Ghghghghgh!" Loesie made a sideways motion in front of her throat.

"Killed? All of them?"

She nodded. Her eyes glittered.

Johanna still hesitated to come any closer. The voice of the Shepherd said in the back of her mind, *They seduce us with what we most want to see.*

Loesie folded her hands in her lap. A tear ran over her cheek and hung at the angle of her jaw. Her shoulders shook.

"Just be strong, all right?" Johanna said. She wanted to hug Loesie, but at the same time, she could *feel* the magic that seeped from her friend.

"I'll come back, I promise. I'll find someone who can—"

"Ghghghghgh!" Loesie pointed out the open door of the barn.

There was a lot of activity of boats in the harbour. From here, you could see the far side of the quay where freight was being unloaded. The Burovian ship still lay there, all the windows and doors closed.

The space where the *Lady Sara* had been yesterday had now been taken by the *Lady Davida*. Adrian walked on the deck.

"What is it, Loesie? What did you see?"

"Ghghghghghgh!" She pointed, but Johanna couldn't make out what she was pointing at. The *Prosperity*, one of the barges belonging to Master Deim, one of Father's friends and competitors, was just coming in. Jakob, Master Deim's sea-cow handler, yelled something to Adrian and Adrian laughed so loud that the sound carried all the way across the harbour to the barn.

"I don't know what you mean, Loesie. I see nothing unusual."

Loesie bent her fingers so that her hands resembled claws and mimicked attacking.

"I don't see any demons," Johanna said. "Why don't I come back this afternoon and bring a slate so that you can draw what you mean?" She should have thought about that earlier.

"Ghghghghghhgh!" Loesie mimicked attacking.

"Yes, I understand."

"Mmmmmmmm!" Loesie shook her head, spreading her hands in a gesture of frustration.

"I'll bring a slate, I promise."

It was only after she had left the barn that Johanna remembered that she had to go to that dratted ball tonight—how could she ever have forgotten that? Maybe she could have some time before leaving?

This stupid ball would be so embarrassing, with her as a dressed-up sugar cake a thousand times less elegant than the girls to whom nobility came as second nature.

She could already hear the scorn as soon as she walked up those palace steps.

She should have stayed with the sea cows.

That dress would have looked nicer on a bitch in heat.

That would be unbearable. She wished the whole thing was already over. Of course the royal family would have no real interest in her. What was Father thinking?

She could, of course, refuse to go, or refuse the dance her father had brokered with the prince, but he was right about one thing. Octavio Nieland should not get the business. Those ships were going to remain under the Brouwer flag.

When she came home, she met Nellie walking up the

stairs carrying a box with a ribbon that would contain the dress Mistress Daphne had adjusted.

"You're just in time for dinner, Mistress Johanna, and then we should get ready."

What, already? What about Loesie? "But the ball is not until tonight."

"Yes, and that will be only just enough time to get everything done."

"The whole afternoon?" But the horrible realisation sank in. Last time she'd gone to a formal occasion—her cousin's wedding—she had also spent ages sitting in her room being primped up by Nellie.

"We need to do your hair, your powder, your jewellery." Nellie counted off on her fingers. "We have a lot to do. The coach comes at six. You have to be ready by then."

But, I promised Loesie . . .

There was no point in resisting. Whatever needed to be done needed to be done.

First Nellie started on Johanna's hair, combed, braided and fluffed it up so it would sit neatly under the beaded hairnet that used to be her mother's. Nellie took forever putting it up in a pile on her head.

Koby brought some tea and biscuits. "Don't eat too much, Mistress. It will look rude if you don't eat at the banquet, and people will gossip."

"People find the silliest things to gossip about."

She gave Johanna an exasperated look.

Then the dress. Nellie helped her do up all the fiddly buttons and hooks and laces at the back.

Nellie brought the pretty box that sat on the dressing table in her bedroom, mostly untouched. Inside, gold and silver chains, gemstones and strings of pearls lay draped over a bed of red velvet. Most of these had been her mother's, pure Estlander silver with precious stones. Johanna felt like a fraud trying on the different pieces. Her mother had been a minor royal, and Johanna was nothing but a fishwife in comparison. She didn't want to meet prince Roald. She knew of the balls, of the infighting between the royal families of neighbouring kingdoms, of the gossip between nobles, and wanted no part of any of it.

Johanna chose her mother's silver necklace with its huge ruby pendant. It lay cool against her skin in the hollow between her breasts.

"Isn't this a bit scandalous?" Johanna asked, putting her hand on the skin of her chest. *So much* skin. Since when had the open and low-cut dresses become the fashion?

"Not if we make your skin all nice again." Nellie draped a cape over Johanna's shoulders to protect the dress from powder. She already had the powder box out, tut-tutting at Johanna's expression. "If you covered your hands in gloves and used an umbrella when going out, you wouldn't get all these horrible freckles and you wouldn't need so much powder." She dusted powder over Johanna's face.

The smell made Johanna's nose tickle.

Then Nellie took the cape off, brushed some hair off the dress and declared Johanna ready to go. She caught sight of herself in the mirror. That young woman in the blue dress with her hair curled and piled in a bun and covered with a gemstone-studded hairnet didn't look like her at all. In fact, she had to move her hand and turn around a fraction just to make sure.

"You look so elegant, Mistress Johanna. You're sure to turn the heads of all the young men at the ball."

Johanna felt like rolling her eyes.

She rose, and found that with the dress' hoops, she could no longer see her feet. When she had tried on the dress with Mistress Daphne, that hadn't been so important, but now

Nellie had to help her down the stairs to make sure that she put her feet on the steps.

Father waited in the hall, dressed in his best silk shirt with ruffled collar and the magnificent purple cloak he'd bought on one of his recent travels. Apparently it was dyed with the pigment of thousands of snails. His hair was tied at the nape of his neck, and he had trimmed his beard. He wore his watch and gold chain and enough perfume that she could smell it halfway down the stairs.

He stared at her, his mouth open.

When Johanna joined him, she noticed a glitter in the corner of his eye.

"You look so much like your mother," he said, his voice unsteady. He cleared his throat and went on, "We went to the ball together a few times. I would be waiting here and she would come down just like you. Looking beautiful. You should wear pretty dresses more often."

Johanna felt uneasy and didn't know what to say. She'd just spent the entire afternoon hating getting dressed up. If it pleased Father, why did she complain?

The rattling of wheels on cobblestones, and the clip-clop of a horse's hooves, drifted in from outside.

"There is the coach." Johanna was glad to break the silence.

He offered her his arm. They left the house and went down the steps and into the street, where people stopped to look. Even though he greeted the people politely, Johanna could feel, beneath his clothes, that Father was nervous, maybe even more so than she was.

She knew the cab driver and his magnificent black horse.

"Good evening, Master and Mistress," the man said. He held the horse by the reins and patted its flank. The animal breathed out through flaring nostrils, tossing its head.

"Nice weather today," the man said.

"That, it is," Father said.

Indeed the sky was cloudless, though less clear than the previous day. The first stars were already visible.

Father helped her up into the cab with the awkward hoops in her dress, climbed in himself, and the driver shut the door while Johanna and her father sat down, facing each other. The driver then walked past the cab and jumped onto the driver's seat. The cab wobbled under his weight and a moment later jerked forwards.

Father stared out the window, pulling at his ruffled sleeves.

"We are not in any kind of trouble, are we?" she asked him when the silence lingered.

He sat with his hands interlaced, elbows leaning on his knees. "We are not, but Saarland is, or, more precisely, the royal family," he said in a low voice. "Johanna, please don't speak of this to anyone else."

"What sort of trouble? Is Estland making threats? Or Burovia?" Most of the inland nations envied Saarland's position, because of its harbour city and the river trade. There had been plenty of threats in the past, but Saarland had been at peace for a long time. She remembered the visions in the wood. Demons crawling through the marshes, unseen to the unsuspecting citizens of the city.

"No threats, as far as I know. Not that sort of trouble." He paused for a bit, looking at the streets glide past out the window. "Or, not that kind of trouble initially."

Why didn't he just say what was going on?

His eyes met hers. Johanna felt chilled with the seriousness in his expression. "The envoy from the King came to us for financial help."

So she'd heard that right. Eavesdropping was really a most useful thing.

"And you named your price for the Brouwer Company's

financial assistance, which was to get me into the palace?" Those words sounded so strange in her mouth.

"No, Johanna." His eyes met hers; then he looked down. "Or maybe yes. One dance with the prince only. There will be others. It still remains the King's choice. But there are a number of important things in your favour: Roald needs to marry as soon as possible. There really is no time to waste. Dare I say the king has already wasted too much time? Secondly, the king has expressed displeasure with the way many of the nobility ridicule the Church and the way he's spent money on it. Most of the nobles are not in his good books."

Not without reason.

"Thirdly, he'll want a woman who goes to church. I think you would be perfectly suited. The royal family doesn't need a pretty princess; they need someone with some common sense in a position where they can make hard decisions. King Nicholaos doesn't seem capable of making these decisions anymore."

"No more wasting money on statues and religious buildings, huh? How does this help the company?"

"You will inherit it and it will remain under your control . . . if you were to be chosen. The queen is the only woman who can inherit in her own right."

"I'll marry the prince, just like that?" She couldn't even believe she was saying this. Why would the royal family have any interest in her?

Father looked at her; there was sadness in his eyes. "Daughter, we need to be strong. Our country needs us. You need to be strong and look after the company. But you can't do it too openly. I wish there was a world where a woman was not bound to her father's or husband's wealth, but there isn't. I can't change that for you."

Johanna looked towards her knees, under the hoops of the

frills. She was angry, angry as she hadn't been for a long time. Angry with herself that she'd been so stupid to expect a free life.

She let a long angry silence pass, but, being who she was, couldn't stay angry for long. There were worse candidates for potential marriage, and even if, as was likely, nothing came of it, she could still say she'd danced with the prince. But the bubble of laughter that rose in her—why on earth would the prince want to dance with her?—quickly evaporated when the coach passed the markets and she remembered Loesie and the demons.

"Did the king say why he wanted to have a bigger army?"

"He wouldn't divulge what happened and why, but the king seems to have deeply upset a Burovian religious order."

"The one that owned the boat and the sanatorium where Roald was?"

"I'm not sure. No one has gone into details about it."

"Does this order belong to the Church of the Triune?"

He held his hands up. "I don't know. What I'm telling you is what the envoy told me. I'm sure there is a lot more to it, but this is all I know. Although I'm guessing you already know a fair bit of it." He met her eyes squarely.

Blood rose to Johanna's cheeks. Outside the cab, the driver yelled at the horse.

"Really, Johanna, if you're going to snoop in the store room, you need to be a lot more careful. You weigh a lot more than when you were eight, you know."

She ignored that comment. "The king wants to put together an army?"

"He is afraid. It seems he did something that made the members of this religious order exceedingly angry. That wouldn't have been such a problem had the order not had strong ties with Baron Uti of Gelre. I understand he is exceedingly angry as well, although he has not publicly expressed his displeasure. Baron Uti is also a guest at the ball. He has probably been invited as a gesture of reconciliation, but the king's envoy let slip through that they don't expect much in the way of negotiation."

"And the king has ignored the army in much of his spending recently," she added.

Father nodded, gravely. "Since Celine's death, the king has lost his grip on pretty much anything, including finances. He's been so consumed by grief that he's spent vast amounts on churches—as if that's going to bring her back—and not enough on things that matter—no, and before you say anything, Johanna, churches do not make any money; they sponge off those who are willing to give it. That could be because they have a lot of money, or because they are somehow deluded that giving to the Church will help them. I suspect the Shepherd promised King Nicholaos salvation for his stricken family, and the king was too addled by grief to see that no one can solve his problems except he himself."

Johanna had often entertained these same thoughts, but hearing them from her father's mouth gave them so much more weight.

Father continued, "That was all fine up until the floods last year, which affected a large part of the royal farms, and the royal family's income from those farms. King Nicholaos did not want to know about it. He sacked the adviser who suggested that they cut spending. Then he neglected to deal with the succession problem."

"Does anyone know why Roald's younger sister was made heir?"

"Roald was sickly. He was not expected to live."

But he did live, and Celine had not. Now he was back, but why was there so much secrecy still? "And now the king wants protection with extra troops? Against priests?"

"Yes, I know, I thought he was crazy, but the envoy said

that it was necessary to protect our borders, which is fair enough, and something that should have been done long ago. I just didn't think that it was worth the level of investment that he wanted. I knew there was something that he wasn't telling me. But something else happened that helps me understand it. I got this today." He reached into his pocket and gave her a crumpled piece of paper that looked like a page torn from an account book. Which, when Johanna unfolded it, was exactly what it turned out to be.

In the neat writing she recognised as belonging to Master Willems, it said,

I have it from sources I can't disclose that there are hostile actions at the border. There are marauding groups of bandits, affiliation unknown, accompanied by creatures that may or may not be demons. They have reportedly invaded farms at the Bend. Their origin is unknown. They are coming in our direction.

Johanna met her father's eyes. They both knew what Master Willems meant—he had seen this on the wind—but his insistence at denying his ability amazed her. At least he had done as she told him.

In a few sentences, Johanna told Father of Loesie and her baskets.

Father knew of Loesie, had met her even, and had never told Johanna to stop seeing her, although he no doubt wished she would. Loesie did not meet the "appropriate lady's companion" standards. The world of willow magic and wind magic was strange to him, but he seemed to understand the need for her to talk to other people with magic, even if those people were a little odd.

Probably Johanna's mother also had the gift of magic, although her father had never explicitly said so. He would have been used to magic. He might even have married her because of that; many river and ocean traders did.

"This is the thing that worries me. There are lots of

rumours about impending attack that seem to have no basis, but when you add up all the stories, the picture becomes quite disturbing. You have seen these demons, and Master Willems has seen them. Your friend has been attacked by them, and had her family killed by them. People like to say that demons don't exist, but things live in those eastern forests that no one has any knowledge of. I've only been into the edges of the forest, but I've heard the murmurings and whisperings in the leaves."

Johanna nodded. She had been with him in that Burovian forest. The thought of that forest still made her shiver, with its gnarled tree trunks and whispering leaves. She still heard the voices, and still felt the fear that they might call her deeper in until she had lost her way.

Father continued, "People from the court say that the king genuinely believed that Celine would rise from the dead. One night, soon after her death, he claimed to have seen her ghost wander the corridors of the palace. He got the Shepherd to do prayer sessions at the spot where he saw her. When that didn't work, he started giving money to the Church. He built a new church. He bought the statue. He encouraged everyone in Saardam to go to church. More prayer would mean more chance that Celine came back."

"But that obviously didn't work either."

Father shook his head and sighed. "It gets very strange after that. The court envoy told me that the king employed an ever-stranger string of people. He said they danced on her grave and performed rituals."

"Was that why a Burovian religious order got involved?"

"I honestly don't know." But it worried him, she could see that.

A chill crept over her back. In her mind, she heard the words of Shepherd Romulus. *You're asking for someone who can perform an exorcism. The Church does not provide these people.*

Exorcisms are quackery that most likely make matters worse than they are. Demons are manifestations of the Triune. They are repelled by prayer, not by fake magicians with horseshoes, goat's blood and other items that wouldn't look out of place in the Lord of Fire's dungeons.

Exorcism, necromancy, both aspects of the darkest corners of magic.

She looked out the window, where the roof of the palace protruded from above the houses.

Would King Nicholaos have been so stupid to have engaged the services of a necromancer? Why, if he was as devout a churchgoer as his behaviour suggested? Why, if his Church forbade any of those dark arts performed by people who were said to have sold their souls to the Lord of Fire? Why, if the king had another child? "If I understand correctly, the king wants to quickly put together a bigger army because he fears trouble with Burovian magicians?"

"That pretty much sums up my conclusions. Another reason why you could be a good choice: your unusual abilities."

Father grabbed her hand and squeezed it, and that was as much a sign of affection as he would ever give her.

CHAPTER 8

A QUEUE of coaches lined up to get into the
forecourt of the palace, a fenced compound
surrounded by gild-topped metal latticework. The
driver whistled for the horse to slow down. The horse seemed
to dislike one of the other horses in the queue. It made
snorting noises and shied sideways. The driver yelled at it,
but that had little effect.

Other horses in the queue also snorted. One of them gave
a soft neigh. From a bit further off came another shout.
"Whoa! Easy, girl, easy."

Father peered out the window. "What's spooking the
horses?"

From her position in the coach, Johanna could see over
the wall to the right of the palace into the garden, an oasis of
tranquillity compared to the forecourt. It was where the king
grew his roses and where water tinkled in mysterious ponds
surrounded by weeping willows. Johanna had been there
once, back in the time when Queen Cygna held *Children's
Day*. Both the prince and his younger sister would have been
there, but she only remembered Celine. She had been

wearing a yellow dress and her mother had to keep telling her not to crawl on the grass. The princess chattered a lot and spoke like Johanna's grandmother, very formal and stiff. Johanna remembered finding it funny, and she remembered not wanting to curtsy for a girl younger than her. It all seemed so painful and awkward now that Celine had been dead two years.

The rose garden now held a gazebo in her memory.

The coach reached the bottom of the steps. With a wobble of the floor and a creak of his leather boots, the driver left his position to open the door.

Father went out first and then helped Johanna, because the awkward dress with its hoops made it impossible for her to see the narrow coach steps.

A huge crowd had assembled near the palace entrance, held back by two lines of stiff-faced guards in Carmine livery. The onlookers were common people who came to watch the latest in fashion and catch up on the juiciest gossip: who went with whom, what who was wearing, that sort of thing.

The sun had just set and a soft glow of candlelight flooded from the porch and main foyer, where Johanna caught glimpses of the genteel folk in colourful garb. She'd been worried that her dress was too exuberantly blue but, judging by the line of noble ladies lined up for the entrance, it looked like bright colours were in fashion this year.

A ripple of surprise went through the crowd when Father took her by the arm and guided her up the steps.

Johanna didn't miss the comments.

"Look, it's Dirk Brouwer and Johanna."

"Isn't that a gorgeous dress that she's wearing?"

Johanna averted her eyes. At least they didn't say *She looks like a dressed-up cow*. But some of them were sure to be thinking that, or worse things like *Did she buy her way into the ball?*

Johanna felt uneasy. Those people on the other side of the line of guards were the ones she'd have to talk to tomorrow about accounts and deliveries of spices and cheese. She wasn't any better than any of them and didn't want to look like she thought she was.

She remembered another visit to the palace, when she was sixteen, the age at which all young women were presented to the King. That had been a most miserable and wet day, in which Carlotta Franzen had slipped and fallen flat on her backside. She now remembered that Prince Roald had been there, and he had rushed forward to help her up. He'd been a gangly youth, and his startling blue eyes had the expression of a frightened rabbit. Blond-haired and still soft-cheeked, the prince had not been unpleasant to look at. Carlotta had been insufferable all afternoon.

On top of the steps a throng of beautifully-primped nobles waited to be allowed into the foyer and hall, the men in rich-coloured suits, the women in frilly dresses, with extravagant hair—some wearing high-heeled shoes on which they could barely walk. Johanna knew most of them. She noticed some daintily raised eyebrows at her and Father's presence.

The palace stood on a low rise and from the top of the steps, you could see over the entire city. To the left were the royal gardens which sloped to the Saar River. Then the harbour and the merchant district with its gabled houses and red roofs. In the distance were the windmills which kept the island on which the city was built above water, and all around, flat land, intersected by silver ribbons of canals. At the horizon there was a lighter-coloured ribbon of sand dunes, but the ocean on the other side remained out of view.

Johanna met the eyes of a young woman who had been looking at her, Carlise d'Agincourt. She had beautiful golden hair held in place with jewelled pins. Her dress was golden with white lace and fitted her narrow waist perfectly. She stood next to an older woman, her mother, who was from the de Weert family but had attained her noble status through her marriage to a Burovian minor royal.

Of course these women were all there for the same reason. Many of them were like her, from families who would not have been the first choice for the prince's bride.

She felt very small. Father seemed so certain that King Nicholaos liked her, but seeing all these beautiful people, she doubted that he would even remember who she was.

A dog started growling and barking. It strained at the leash held by one of the palace guards. A woman lower on the steps squealed. In the forecourt, a coach horse neighed, and then another one. More dogs started barking. Men shouted orders.

Someone behind Johanna said, "He shouldn't have brought the stupid animal. It spooks the horses."

The woman who had squealed was Gertrude Hendricksen, one of the guests. She was here with her father, and he, of course, had the monkey on his shoulder.

Guess that explained why the horses were so nervous. Johanna shivered, although the evening was quite warm.

Finally they entered the foyer with its chandeliers and stained glass windows and smooth mosaic floor with the Carmine House's crest—the rooster—in stone of various shades of brown. It was noisy in here, with talk echoing back from the ceiling. Chamber music floated in through the open doors which led into what was called the garden room, a big and luscious hall, where all official functions were held.

A courtier came to take Johanna's overcoat and Father led her into the hall. The dais with the king's, queen's and prince's chairs was at the far end. A long table had been set up here, with a pristine white tablecloth and precious gold-rimmed plates and crystal glasses. A chamber orchestra played at the bottom of the steps to the dais. More groups of dressed-up noble guests stood here and there on the floor.

If the royal family was in some kind of trouble, this hall definitely showed no sign of it.

Long tables with glittering silverware were set around the perimeter of the room, tables groaning with delicate porcelain, crystal glasses, carafes of wine, gold tableware and dainty candle holders with slender white candles. Servants were carrying in trays of exquisite canapés, fancy cheeses and unfamiliar fruit, and covered dishes with huge silver lids that left wonderful smells in their wake.

No one was dancing yet. People stood talking in knots of garishly-coloured costumes, ruffled collars and fluffed-up hair, in a display of the latest Lurezian fashion. Johanna hated to think of how much money in clothing, footwear, hats and jewellery was walking around on the dance floor. That was probably her merchant upbringing talking.

All these women must have spent the entire day in front of the mirror. The scents of heavy perfume and powder threatened to overwhelm her. What was she doing here? This was not how Father had brought her up. This was not the type of life she wanted.

A couple of nobles deep in discussion burst out in laughter as Johanna and her father passed. Amongst them stood Octavio Nieland, a tall imposing figure. He wore his dark hair in a ponytail, sleek and simple. His shirt was quality silk, cream-coloured, with simple ruffles, and his overcoat was dark blue. He held a long-stemmed glass with a be-ringed hand. He met Johanna's eyes over the rim of his glass. His eyebrows rose.

"Johanna, how nice of you to join us." It sounded like *what on Earth are you doing here?*

He gave a little bow. "We must have a dance later tonight."

Johanna shivered. This man was beating down Father's door to ask her hand in marriage?

The people in his group had stopped taking and all looked at her. His sister Julianna was there, in a dress very similar to the pink dress Mistress Daphne had shown Johanna. Except it looked stunning on her. Julianna Nieland, of course, had the figure of a lady, the wide hips and the narrow waist.

Her skin was also naturally pale, not ugly and freckled like Johanna's, and the red paint on her lips and the blushes on her cheeks had been applied with a subtle and delicate hand, and probably not by the maid. The others in the group were their cousins, the young men in colourful trousers and jackets with high-heeled boots and frilled shirts, the young women all dressed up like sugar cakes and acting as if it came natural to them.

Father led Johanna away from the group, giving a polite bow to Lady Suzanna Nieland, who must be well into her seventies by now. The lady regarded the newcomers over her monocle with an expression of curiosity.

"What a bunch of empty-headed peacocks," Father muttered, and he didn't seem to be overly concerned about whether or not the Nielands were within earshot.

Whether they were or not, or whether the surreal sweet strains of music drowned out Father's words, Johanna could still feel their gazes prick in her back when she and Father reached the other side of the hall. One thing she knew for certain: Octavio Nieland didn't want to marry her. He wanted to own the Brouwer Company. She would be an unfortunate part of the bargain and would probably be treated as such.

On the other side of the hall, Father found a group of his colleagues, older, grizzled company owners, captains and other men of boats. The men, merchants or minor nobles, were from mixed heritage, as was common amongst merchanting families. Many of the well-off citizens from all the surrounding countries sent their sons to Saardam to work. Johanna had seen most of them before, and knew all their names. The way they stood slightly apart from the nobles and other guests made it clear that they were also not regular guests at occasions like this. The king had really cast his invitations wide this year.

There was the half-Lurezian Captain Murain who traded fabrics up and down the rivers. With him was his Estlander wife, Lora, a short rotund woman who was the opposite of what Johanna imagined her mother to have been like. She laughed a lot but spoke with such a terrible accent that Johanna had trouble understanding her.

There was the Estlander merchant, Master Deim, whose brother lived in Saardam and who owned seagoing ships and was in partnership with a Saarlander noble family to crew and kit out the ships. He was a man of tall tales, and only interrupted his current story, about foreign ships shadowing his brother's, to greet Johanna and her father exuberantly.

With his soft face and friendly eyes, Master Deim was one of these people hard to dislike, but oh, he was such a chatterbox.

The other men greeted her father with claps on the shoulder, and bows to Johanna, calling her sincere but laughworthy names, like fair lady and golden maiden. She guessed it came with their eastern and southern heritage, because those people were always more pompous. But they were also more open and generous with compliments.

Not used to this kind of male attention, Johanna found it a bit embarrassing.

She remained next to her father, listening to their laughter and familiar tales, normally spun in the comfort of her father's study. Master Deim, already red-faced from the wine, leaned closer to her than necessary. "You know, if your father is going to invest in seafaring ships, he'll need to buy protection. There are many lands beyond the Horn, but not all of them are friendly."

She nodded politely. Each year several ships went missing in seas past the Horn. The land route to the silk-country was much more reliable, and shorter. Yet there was much more glamour associated with the high seas. Sailors who left and returned safely were celebrated as heroes. Something lived on the other side of the Horn that did not like other people coming there. There were tales of monstrous creatures, sea serpents and dragons. Ships went missing each year.

A servant came past with a tray of glasses and Master Deim was the first to take one. Johanna took a glass, too.

He lifted his to her and took a good swig. "Might as well enjoy the good life while it lasts."

"While it lasts?" His words sent her heart into a rapid beat. Had he seen ill omens on the wind? Johanna could usually sense if a person had magic. Master Deim had not struck her as such a person, but then again, sometimes people surprised her.

He laughed. "Last time I went drinking, the wife locked all the doors on me and I sat all night in the street. Cold, it was, too. So this time, I've been smart and I'll sleep in the barn. At least all those cow ladies do is fart in the water." He laughed again, a rolling belly laugh that, no matter the sad rumours surrounding his marriage, made Johanna laugh as well.

Sea cows farted. A lot. Bubbles in the water. The image of Master Deim sleeping in his finery amongst the harnesses and bags of potatoes next to the bubbly water was priceless.

She should calm down about Loesie's warning. So far, there was no proof that any of it was true. The willow wood did not usually lie, but Loesie was clearly possessed by something evil, and anything she had touched should be treated with suspicion.

Master Deim's face turned serious. "You know, between you and me, I worry about my wife's churchgoing. I think I've been a good person all my life. Paid all my dues and never harmed anyone. Gave a whole lot of poor buggers jobs who would've starved otherwise. What right does this Shepherd have to say that we are bad people? We are not, and this country has prospered because of us."

"I understand," Johanna said, but she felt uneasy. Did *us* mean merchants or people who had magic? Magic that was more common in people from the east, like him, and like her mother?

Many of the Brouwer company deck hands, too, were refugees or ex-mercenaries from eternal petty conflicts on the eastern Estland border. People there starved to death, so the lucky ones came to prosperous Saardam where they hauled sacks of potatoes or cheeses all day, and could afford to feed their families.

She looked away, and noticed Octavio Nieland observing her from the other side of the hall. His intense expression sent a chill down her back. Dark and brooding, Nellie called it. Others called him handsome, but all those descriptions were just different words for *bully* to her. There was no way she would ever agree to marry him.

She turned away from him, back to Master Deim and his uncomfortable conversation, but could still fell Octavio's gaze pricking at the back of her head.

Father was talking to another merchant on Johanna's other side. He gave the appearance of being relaxed but she could see that he was nervous, with his thumbs jammed in his belt. He wasn't drinking. "Gerald, have you met my daughter, Johanna?"

"No, I have not." The fellow was grey-haired, with a short, neatly-clipped beard. He wore a long, elegant coat and a simple white shirt. No lace. He took Johanna's hand. "My pleasure, madame."

"You're Burovian?" She recognised his accent.

"Yes, indeed, I am. How did you guess?" He laughed.

"He's the captain of the ship that brought Roald back," Father said, his voice full of meaning.

Whoa, did he belong to the religious order that the king was said to have offended?

The man laughed. "Not sure if you'll thank me for it, but it's true, lady."

"And how are things in Burovia?" Johanna studied his clothes, but could see no sign that this man was a monk.

"As good as can be." There was meaning in those words, too, but Johanna had no idea what he was trying to say.

He smiled as if she knew what he was talking about.

Johanna turned to her father, but he was talking to the merchant next to him. So she chatted to the Burovian merchant, but became none the wiser about his mysterious remarks.

Looking around the circle of her father's acquaintances, all well-to-do merchants and boat people in their fineries, it struck her that there was a reason Father had joined these men: they were all from outside the city and they would either have magic or employ someone who did. None of them belonged to the Church of the Triune.

As potential bride to the prince, she was their spearhead: religious enough on the surface to be attractive to the royal family, but ultimately loyal to them. If the choice was Church or magic, Johanna would have no choice but to choose magic. Magic went with merchants and people who owned boats. She was their pawn, their puppet, their spearhead into destroying the influence of the Church in Saardam so that they could conduct their business freely along the rivers regardless of borders. Why hadn't she seen this coming earlier?

Her head reeled.

At that moment, a fanfare of trumpets blasted into the crowd. Conversations dissolved, groups split up and people lined up on both sides of the hall.

CHAPTER 9

DAZED AS SHE WAS, Johanna ended up a couple of rows back in the crowd.

Two rows of King's Heralds lined up on both sides of the aisle.

First to come into the hall was the king's speaker, carrying the staff. Then followed King Nicholaos, wearing his Carmine cloak. The circlet on his head crowned his severe, bearded face. She hadn't seen him close up for a while, and thought that grief over his daughter's death had aged him terribly. His hair used to be ashen blond, but it had gone grey. His skin had never been good, but now it resembled the colour of dirty linen. His cheeks looked hollow.

Queen Cygna walked behind him. Not even the occasion of the ball had convinced her to change out of the black dress and veil she had worn since Celine's death. She looked down as a prisoner being led to the gallows, with her face mostly hidden in the shadow of the black lace.

Behind them followed a tall and thin young man with short-cropped blond hair and a short blond beard. The way Prince Roald walked—stiff and staring at his father's back—

made him look ill at ease and awkward. Since Johanna had last seen him, he had changed so much that she didn't think she would have recognised him if she'd met him in the street dressed in civilian clothes.

Two ladies in the crowd behind Johanna whispered that he looked well, and he did, but he did not wave, raise his head or talk to anyone the entire way through the hall. He looked petrified of all this attention he was getting.

What if he was painfully shy and was looking forward to dancing with primped-up, hopeful girls just as little as some girls were?

Behind the royal family followed a procession of minor royals and guests. Of course there was Princess Josafina of Estland, in the dark red of the Aroden house. She wore her hair piled on top of her head like a giant dome, and Johanna wondered how much of it was real. She was a cousin to the king who, failing a husband or a country to rule, had made Saardam her permanent home.

The couple of boys trailing her were presumably some of the Estlander baron's six sons who had been sent to their aunt for education.

Behind them walked a bearded man dressed in black leather. He was at least a head taller than Princess Josafina, and his beard, huge and bushy, covered the top of his chest above his considerable belly. He wore his hair, brown and curly and greying at the temples, in a loose ponytail. His arms, mostly bare save for the jerkin's very short sleeves, rippled with muscles and bore more scars than those of the average sea cow handler.

Johanna had never seen Baron Uti of Gelre before, but this man fitted the descriptions that went around of him. He was said to have been a fierce warrior in his younger days and still looked the part. His expression was curious rather than angry, but he would no doubt be a force to be reckoned with if he was upset. With him were Master Lanston, ambassador from Estland, and two men in long Burovian capes she had never seen before. People from this religious order?

The Rede River separated Gelre and Burovia. Both were thickly-forested countries and one of Gelre's main towns, Florisheim, lay opposite the Burovian town of Velsdam. Apparently, the river was small enough to cross by barge at that point so there was a lot of contact between the two towns.

On the other side of the Estlander ambassador walked a man with rust-red curls down to his shoulders. He wore brown woollen trousers and a white, long-sleeved shirt and a leather jerkin embossed with some kind of sigil. He looked exotic and foreign, not proper at all, with that long hair and his strange clothing.

He was talking to the ambassador, and as he walked past, his eyes met Johanna's in the crowd. His eyes were brown, his chin strong and smoothly shaven. The corner of his mouth went up a fraction.

A shiver crawled over Johanna's back. Magic, as strong as she'd ever felt it. It radiated from him.

The procession went up to the dais, where Queen Cygna and Prince Roald took their positions on either side of the King's chair and all the other royals and guests found their places on the table behind and to the sides of the royal family. The red-haired man ended up at the back where Johanna couldn't see him anymore, although the touch of magic still made her skin prick.

She clamped her arms around herself. If people from the east had magic as strong as that, what hope would there be for Saarland to defend itself in case of a conflict? Especially if the Church started banishing people with magic?

A serious-looking man in a Carmine coat had taken up a position behind the prince's chair. Johanna wondered who he was—apart from a member of the royal family's courtiers—and what he was doing there, because no one else had a personal minder.

Another trumpet fanfare signalled that the royal family was seated.

All the guests now filed past the dais, where each one bowed or curtsied to the king. Johanna and her father lined up with Master Deim and the other merchants.

Slowly the line shuffled forwards.

When Johanna and her father's turn came, the king looked at Father and gave a barely perceptible nod that made Johanna's heart race. What had these men been negotiating behind her back? Prince Roald sat in a stiff position, staring into the back of the hall. He didn't look at anyone or talk to anyone. His foot jiggled.

On the other side of the dais, the queue dissolved and guests broke off into pairs or little groups which scattered across the floor. Johanna and her father stopped to look back at the dais, where guests still filed past.

"What do you think?" Father said in a low voice.

She glanced at Prince Roald, who was still jiggling his foot. "He seems frightened."

"Frightened? I would have thought he was bored."

"Wouldn't you be frightened if you were told to pick a girl out of all these dressed-up dolls, and you knew none of them?"

"He should be used to being the centre of attention."

Should was an easy word, but nothing was as it should. Roald looked healthy enough. Why had the king shielded him so? "Did the king tell you what's wrong with him and why he had to be sent away?"

"He has a very fragile personality."

Did that justify the special treatment? Then something else occurred to her. "Does he have magic?"

Father's eyes met hers squarely. "They say magic might have had something to do with it."

"But magic would make him more suited to the job. Think of all the things I know because of the magic in the wood." And magic didn't give a person a *fragile personality*, whatever that might mean. When it came to the prince, people spoke in impenetrable metaphors.

"What would the Shepherd have to say about a prince with magic?"

True. And religious as King Nicholaos was, that could be a problem. She glanced at the prince again. When meeting someone for the first time, she usually had at least a suspicion if someone had magic. Like Master Diem. She felt that with Master Willems, too, and Loesie. She had felt nothing when Roald passed her, but he might have been overshadowed by the red-haired man behind him, and Johanna tried very hard not to think of that chilling look in those brown eyes.

It was a mystery.

By now, the line to greet the king had dissolved.

A bell rang. The king rose from his seat and motioned for silence. The music stopped, and chatter and laughter died.

Roald remained in his chair, looking at the ground. His mother leaned across the empty chair between them and said something. He jerked his head up.

"Thank you all for being here with us today," the king said. "Today, our annual ball, is a great occasion. As you will have seen, Prince Roald has joined us in this occasion. He has recently returned to Saardam and will be taking up his duties as crown prince shortly. No doubt that's why we see such a wonderful presence from all the young ladies today. There will be a few words from my son later on, but for now I trust that you will amuse yourselves without my interfering. Enjoy the sounds of the orchestra and the wonderful dishes from our trusted cook. Feast and be merry."

The orchestra struck up a waltz that went with a dance called the dandelion. It was a light and frivolous tune, designed for a circle of friends, but Johanna danced it with Father. He wasn't a bad dancer, but he trod on her toes several times. It was crowded, and he was no doubt thinking about other matters. Then the herald called out for a change of partner, and she lost him in the crowd. She danced with a merchant's son, then a nobleman with bad breath and then decided to get something to eat at the tables around the perimeter of the room, where she found Master Deim in a heated discussion with a group of merchants.

"He's asked Dirk Brouwer," one of the men was saying.

"He came to me, too," another man said. "Asked me to contribute for the good of the country. He was not at all clear about what had happened that warrants such an expansion of the army. King's orders, he said, but you know what? I think the King is seeing things that aren't there."

"Don't know about that," Master Deim said. Oh yes, Johanna was right about him feeling magic. She didn't know if it was wind or wood, but it was definitely there.

"Who is about to invade us, then? Where will these people come from? I've been up and down the Saar and Rede Rivers as far as one can go, and I've seen no proof of any hostilities."

"It's not something you can see," Master Deim said.

The other merchant's eyes went wide. "It's a magical thing?"

"Shhh!" another said.

Then they whispered to each other, and Johanna could no longer hear them.

She went to stand closer, but at that moment, the music stopped and King Nicholaos took to the podium once more, and everyone fell silent.

"As you have seen, tonight is the joyous event that our

dear son has again joined us, ready to begin his duties as crown prince. I present to you, my son Roald."

The young man rose and the crowd cheered, rather half-heartedly, Johanna thought. His father placed his hand on his shoulder and guided him to face the people. The king whispered in his ear. Roald nodded and King Nicholaos retreated.

Roald stared into the crowd, his eyes unfocused.

And stared. His lips moved, but no sound came out.

He scrunched up the hem of his tunic with white-knuckled hands.

Some whispers rose in the gathered audience and someone behind Johanna let out a nervous chuckle.

"Um—welcome to the palace," Roald finally managed to say. His voice was pleasant, but didn't undo the unsettling effect of that too-long silence.

"Welcome," he said again. "Um . . . thank you all for coming. I think it's time for dancing now . . ." He looked over his shoulder.

King Nicholaos went to his rescue. "You will be aware that Roald is interested in the young ladies of our fair city, and we have invited some of them here. Ladies, you may all come forward and line up."

He guided his son down the stairs to the dais. The man who had been standing behind Roald's chair followed the pair. "Ladies, ladies," he called out. "Please line up here so that I can tick off your name from the list."

"Here you go, daughter." Father gave Johanna a tiny push in the back.

About twenty young women had already formed a line. Julianna Nieland, in her pink dress, was one of them. She gave Johanna another one of her "what are you doing here?" raised-eyebrow looks that seemed to be permanently plastered on her face when Johanna was around.

Johanna turned away from her. She wanted no prince,

but to have Julianna Nieland snatch the prince's favour instead would be insufferable. That would be like being sixteen all over again and watching Carlotta Franzen strut around like a peacock because the prince helped her up when she fell.

Roald faced the group. He held his back unnaturally straight, and kept looking to the side, but his father was talking to the courtier with the list. The man proceeded to call out each girl's name and marked her off as if she was an item in a delivery.

While the orchestra played softly, Roald and his father inspected the line. King Nicholaos made small talk with the girls, and each curtsied. Johanna was sweating under her gown. Why on earth was she doing this? It was like being a cow for sale at the markets.

In the middle of the soft musical tones, there was a loud discordant twang.

Conversations stopped. People turned their heads to the orchestra.

From in the middle of the seated musicians, the lutist rose, his face red. One of the strings on his instrument dangled loose.

He stammered, "Um, I'm sorry, my string . . ."

In that moment of silence, Roald let out a giggle. He arched his back and clapped his hands. "Hehehehehee! That's so funny!"

His voice echoed through the hall and made the hair on Johanna's neck stand up.

Master Hendricksen sometimes brought his monkey when he came to talk to Father. It sat on his shoulder, as it did tonight; and when it got excited it made a sound like that.

The King tried to get his son to shut up, but Prince Roald laughed and laughed. No one else was laughing. The faces of the noble ladies showed expressions of horror. One woman at the front of the crowd gestured for her daughter in the queue to come back to her.

On the dais, Queen Cygna sat as stone, staring at the other side of the hall. Johanna could see her dead-faced expression through her veil.

In the eerie silence, the King said, his face unemotional. "After that—um—interlude, I think the orchestra needs some time to fix up the—um—problems, but we can proceed without music."

But no one could dance without music, and the lack of music made uncomfortable moments so much more awkward.

Murmurs broke out throughout the hall. A lady behind Johanna whispered to her neighbour, "He's not good in the head. No wonder they've kept him hidden for so long."

Another said, "Pity the girl who gets to marry him."

"Oh, you're only saying that because you have no daughters. A prince is a prince. All young women want to marry a prince."

"Look then. Magda has already withdrawn her daughter."

It was true. The girl in question stood with her mother. She was talking and gesturing angrily and wiping her eyes. Black kohl had smudged over her cheek.

The lute player ran across the hall with his instrument and a new string and re-settled in the orchestra.

Soon, the music started again. A servant with a tray of drinks went up the dais and offered the first one to Queen Cygna, but she refused. When the servant had gone to the guests, she lifted her veil and dabbed at her eyes.

Johanna didn't know where to look. This was all so embarrassing and deeply horrible. Johanna could imagine the pain. The young Princess Cygna, youngest daughter of the king of the northern land of Scandia, married off at her sixteenth birthday to a crown prince she had never met of a country where she had never been, pregnant the same night. By all accounts, Roald's birth had been long and difficult, not in the least because of Cygna's young age, and all for nothing. The prince would never be suitable to rule a country. Many diseases could be cured, but those in the head were forever.

There was some action in the line. Out of all the girls, the prince managed to pick out Julianna Nieland. The king took her hand and put it in his son's. She looked terrified.

Roald led her into the middle of the dance floor. He walked stiffly, but Julianna appeared to waver, and her face was so white that it looked like she might faint.

The music began. Roald was a stiff, clumsy dancer, and trod on Julianna's feet several times. He spoke to her a few times, and Julianna arched her back further and further from him.

Normally, Johanna would have felt vindicated if Julianna embarrassed herself, but this was beyond embarrassment.

Then all of a sudden, she screamed, wrenched herself from Roald's grip and ran across the dance floor where she threw herself in her mother's arms, crying. Lady Suzanna Nieland stood too far from Johanna to hear any of what they said.

The girls around Johanna craned their necks.

"What happened?"

"What did he say to her?"

Julianna was still crying on her mother's shoulder. Her brother patted her back. Lady Nieland cast the king a disapproving look.

"Johanna Brouwer," King Nicholaos announced.

Johanna had been looking at the Nieland family, and returned her attention to the king, heart thudding.

"My son wishes to have a dance with you."

Too late to back out. Roald met her eyes with a small frown.

Johanna took his hand and curtsied, first to the king and then the prince, but her mind felt blank, as if she was in a very bad dream. Had Father known what state Roald was in? *Magic might have something to do with it.* What nonsense.

Roald was a halfwit, and Father would have known that. That showed what he thought of her: a chess piece that he could use to advance the business. The anger made her even hotter under the stifling dress.

But she would rather die than make a scene like Julianna Nieland. She would dance with him in a dignified way. Whatever he said to Julianna was nothing that Johanna wouldn't have heard before. She spoke to the ships' boys and deck hands. She heard their swearing. She knew where they went after work, and because those ladies, if they deserved that term, always knew who of their regular clients was out of work, Johanna spoke to them as well. Helena from the harbour-side bar was not a bad person. She and her friends were useful and, like Mistress Daphne, full of gossip. Nothing the prince could say to her would make her scream and run off.

Sure enough when she raised her head, it was to find Roald looking at her. At her chest, to be more precise. At the point where the small groove between her breasts vanished under the dress.

"Roald, now behave yourself," the king said.

Roald giggled. "Oooh, I like this one. I get all the good girls today, don't I?"

"Yes, but don't say anything rude." King Nicholaos gave a forced smile. "Go on, then, show her your dancing skills."

"I think I like this ball after all."

Roald took Johanna's hand. His hand was sweaty and when he faced her in the middle of the dance floor, his breath stank of liquor. From close up, his face had a ruddy complexion and his skin was flaky. Probably from spending too much time inside.

The orchestra started to play a dance that was called the prince's waltz, a slow dance with quite complicated steps.

"You are very pretty." His eyes were still uncomfortably focused on her breasts.

"Um, thank you, Your Highness."

He laughed, loudly. "Heheheheee! You hear that? She got it right, Mother!"

On the dais, Queen Cygna did her best to pretend she wasn't there.

"Shall we start dancing. . . ?" She almost said *Your Highness* again to set him off a second time. Instead she pulled him into a move she hoped was a waltz, but she seemed to have totally forgotten the steps.

Roald was clumsy. He stepped on her feet several times, and kneed her in the thigh once. He couldn't do turns. Everyone was watching and Johanna didn't know where to look.

Roald was oblivious to the attention. "My mother says I have to ask you questions. Do you like questions?"

What to reply to that? "Um . . ."

He was still staring at her breasts, leaning over and peeking into her dress, as far as he could go without touching. Johanna was overcome by a desire to run out of the room, but she reminded herself that she wasn't going to make a scene like Julianna Nieland.

"I don't like the questions Mother wants me to ask."

"Shhh. You can ask questions, but you don't want everyone to hear them, Your—um—what would you like to know?"

"Oooh, secret questions. I like that."

All around the hall, the nobles were looking on, their faces stiff in horror and secret fascination, pretending this wasn't happening. Pretending that they didn't see the prince staring at her breasts. She could already hear the comments *She shouldn't have worn that scandalous thing, cheap try-hard that she is.*

"Do you like gingerbread biscuits?" Roald asked.

"Yes, I like gingerbread biscuits." For some reason, she thought about Loesie, who would be wondering where she was. "Our cook makes very good ones."

"I don't like gingerbread biscuits."

"Oh, I'm sorry to hear that."

He laughed his high-pitched laugh again, oblivious that everyone was staring at him.

And then he said, giving a look at his father, "My father wants me to ask you why you want to marry me." He bent close to her ear and she could smell the liquor again.

He waited for effect, and then said, "But I'm not going to ask that."

"You aren't?" At this point, she was reacting with the sole purpose to survive this dance without upsets.

"Oh, you want to tell me anyway?" He bent closer again. His alcohol-laced breath tickled the bare skin on her chest.

She almost gagged and had to restrain herself not to rip herself out of his grip, which was surprisingly strong.

"I'd like to know."

She was dizzy; she panicked. She didn't know what she was doing, thinking nothing but that she *had* to get out of his grip or he'd do something embarrassing to her under the eyes of all these people.

"I don't really want to marry you." What else could she say? She couldn't do this. She couldn't. Her father couldn't honestly expect her to shackle herself to a crazy man.

He retreated and nodded. "Good. Because I don't want to marry you either. Your tits are too small."

And with that, he stepped back, gave a mock bow and

turned away. Johanna walked away as fast as she could without running. The king gestured his son that he needed to go back to the waiting line of girls. Roald crossed his arms over his chest and said something, to which his father grabbed his shoulder and spoke to him sternly.

Roald squealed, "I don't want to!"

And King Nicholaos spoke to him more sternly.

The people around the dance floor watched this exchange with morbid curiosity displayed on their faces.

Only three girls remained of the original twenty. All three were nobles, with white faces and wide eyes. Johanna would have grinned at them if she hadn't felt so awful.

To her horror, Father was right behind her. She met his eyes squarely.

"I can't—"

He took her by the arm and dragged her off to the side of the room, under the arched gallery, where the light was dim and only a lone palace guard watched.

At the same time as Johanna began with, "I'm sorry, but —" he said, "Johanna . . ." There was a tone of warning in his voice.

And then they were both silent.

"I can't do this," she said, eventually. "I'm sure you understand."

"Shhh. Johanna, this is a great opportunity."

"Marrying an idiot?" She fought to keep tears out of her voice. What did he think she was? "Did you know about this?"

"Think about it, Johanna. In a number of years' time, I will be dead. King Nicholaos and Queen Cygna will be dead. If he survives that long, Roald is too simple to govern our country. Who does that leave in power other than the prince's wife?"

"I don't care. You didn't answer my question. Did you know about this?"

"It is a wonderful opportunity for us."

Johanna stared at him, the horror of what he said coming over her. He wasn't going to answer the question, because he had known. He was simply using her as a piece in a game. "I thought you loved me."

"I do, and I don't know what else to do for you. You want freedom and power, I give you freedom and power."

"Not like this."

"Then there will be no option but for me to agree to give you to Octavio Nieland." His face was hard.

"No. You don't understand anything. I will not be given to anyone. I'm happy to remain a spinster for the rest of my life. Listen to what I say for once: I don't want to get married to anyone."

She turned on her heel and ran away from him.

CHAPTER 10

ALL OF A SUDDEN, Johanna found the hall too hot and too noisy. The smell of sweat mingled with perfume and food made her feel dizzy. The tight bodice of the dress constricted her breathing. Everyone seemed to be looking at her, and those haughty noble faces carried expressions of pity. She could hear their mocking voices. *Poor simple girl. She really didn't know what she let herself in for, didn't she?*

She pushed herself through the crowd until she came to the side of the hall.

Through a set of double doors, she ended up in the gallery that ran between the hall and the garden, a long corridor, with on the right-hand side doors that led into the hall. Muffled sounds of talk and laughter and music filtered through the closed doors. Moonlight slanted in through the arched windows on the left.

She stopped in front of one of those windows, seeing the beautifully sculpted garden and the golden statue of the Triune through a haze of tears.

She'd gone and undone all of Father's hard negotiating work. He had every right to be furious with her.

And of course he was right. She was his only heir. If she didn't marry, the company would stop with her. If she could put up with Roald, it was the best position for her to be in. The king seemed to like her. Roald probably didn't have much of a say in it. Pretty much like herself. All she needed to do was . . . She shuddered at the thought of letting him touch her.

What was Father thinking?

She stood in front of the window bathed in pale moonlight, clamping her arms around herself and calming herself by leaning her forehead against the window. The glass fogged up where she breathed on it. She didn't know what to do, and what she'd say to Father. She would have to apologise, but she wanted an apology from him, too. She might even have agreed to a meeting with the prince had he told her what was going on.

The sense of betrayal stung worse than anything else. That her father would *sell* her without telling her.

That's what you get for failing to grow up, said the little voice that sounded like Nellie. Grown-up girls got married, plain and simple.

If she *had* to marry right now, she would choose . . . Master Willems. At least he knew how the business worked and wouldn't want anything out of the deal other than to keep his job.

Yes.

It was silly. And impossible. He was just a shopkeeper's son. And he was heavily involved in the Church. He probably didn't even like her. She trusted him, and that was more than could be said for any other candidates.

She didn't want to get married.

The way Roald stared at her breasts made her shudder.

This was a dreadful place and not one where she belonged. Loesie would be wondering where she was. She'd be hungry. Maybe she'd go wandering around the docks, with all the problems that would bring.

In the middle of the floor of the gallery was a large plain slab of marble with a carved inscription. Four pillars marked the corners, each with a candle on a sconce. A faint breeze made the flames flap, casting moving shadows over the stone.

Johanna pushed herself away from the window and walked over. The inscription on the marble slab said,

Born from dust, return to dust,

with underneath a name.

At the tender age of nineteen. Our beloved princess Celine Maraina Hestia Carmine de Lacoeur van Leeuwen.

No one ever listed all the royal family's names and titles. You needed a whole page for that.

Celine, felled suddenly by a deadly infection. Celine, younger sister to Roald. Celine, first heir to the Carmine Throne.

Johanna remembered hearing the news of her death. She remembered the day of her funeral, how queen Cygna had broken down and collapsed on the dais. She remembered the king's silent and emotionless appearance.

She remembered the talk about Roald and the speculation about his absence.

There had been whispers that he'd been glad she was dead. Some even said that he might have killed his sister. No one understood why he had been passed over for the throne anyway, although the reason for choosing Celine was widely rumoured to be to attract local princes in marriage, influential princes from large kingdoms. But the royal family had never confirmed this rumour. They hadn't married Celine off as soon as she turned sixteen either. Knowing what Johanna knew now, it all made sense. The Carmines were a dangerously small family and they carried a curse that was worse than that of magic: that of madness. Potential suitors would find out about Roald, and would worry about any children Celine might have. That would have repelled a lot of potential candidates, especially those from other royal families. They'd been marrying each other's cousins for so many generations that no royal family was unrelated to the other royal families.

Add to that the fact that King Nicholaos had made himself unpopular with the nobility of the surrounding lands by giving the Church of the Triune legal status, and you had a problem. A big problem.

And because of Celine, Johanna stood here. Because of Celine, she had failed her father.

She buried her face in her hands.

A voice behind her said, "Lady."

Johanna gasped and turned around. "Who's there?"

"It's only me." From the shadows of the porch came the red-haired man she had seen with the king's guests. He bowed. "Excuse me very much, my lady. I seem to have startled you. That was not my intention. I merely sought the way to the garden. I'm quite hot." He spoke with a curious accent.

"Oh . . . Down that way, I think." She pointed half-heartedly to the end of the passage.

From close up, the prick of magic was so strong that it made the hairs on her arms stand on end. What kind of magic was it? Not willow magic because that was much more subtle. Not wind magic or he would follow the way to the garden by the guidance of the breeze. If she was to have any chance of finding out, she needed to touch his bare skin. His arms were mostly covered by long flowing sleeves. His hands were long-fingered, but hands were really not much good for magic transmission. Hands touched too many other things that they easily became contaminated.

His neck . . . She stared at the way the light danced in his hair. Felt that most horrible of feelings creep up on her: a blush. Fortunately, it would be too dark for him to notice.

"I don't think we've been introduced, my lady, my name is Kylian, prince of Gelre."

"Baron Uti's son?" Her voice sounded small and immature to her ears.

"The very one." He bowed.

"I'm afraid I can't compete with that. My name is Johanna Brouwer."

"Oh, the famous merchant's daughter."

"You know me?" Surely he said that to humour her.

"Who hasn't heard of the famous Brouwer river barges? They bring spices and tobacco all up and down the inland towns. And you were dancing with the prince just now. Your name was whispered all over the hall."

"Um . . ." Johanna was going to say *not in a good way, probably*, but that would lead to all sorts of conversations she didn't want to have. Also, it made sense that he'd know Father's ships, important as the river trade was to the inland towns, but she had no idea why he would know her. She wasn't famous at all. She had been to Lurezia once with her father, but no one knew the Brouwer Company there, except other merchants, whom Father had spent ages talking to. To the fourteen-year-old Johanna, it was nothing but a big, strange city that stank, where no one spoke her language.

In the hall, the orchestra struck up a tune called The Swan that involved a dance where the man held the woman by the elbows from behind and the pair moved across the dance floor in an elegant glide.

He bowed again. "Lady Johanna, I would be most pleased to have this dance." He held his arms ready.

"Um . . . Isn't the dance floor in the hall?" Except she didn't really want to go back there, not to watch the embarrassing spectacle of petrified girls dancing with Roald if there were still any girls left who wanted to try, or to see Roald throw more tantrums, or see Father's pained face.

Johanna felt like an idiot. She was turning into another version of Nellie, always worrying about this or that and what people thought of it. Nellie never had any *fun*. And Johanna's life was not much fun at the moment. What happened to the girl who two days ago danced down the church steps wearing clogs?

Kylian was handsome, and smiled at her with quiet intelligence. Not the predatory look of Octavio Nieland. Not the dumb look of Prince Roald. Not the expectant looks of all the nobles. Or the suspicious looks of anyone who knew about magic.

What was the harm of one dance? She had danced with plenty of young men at other occasions, albeit none as formal as this one. After tonight, he would go back to the baron's castle. She would go back to being plain Johanna and she would never see him again.

But there is no one else here, the annoying little voice in her head said.

She forced that little voice to shut up and put her hands in his. His palms felt warm and dry. Pleasant, not at all like Roald's sweaty hands.

And his magic—whoa! It swept her up in a maelstrom of visions, of his home, the town of Florisheim by the Rede River. She saw the castle high above the roofs of the town, with a forbidding entrance, a fat round tower on which flew the flag of the barony.

He turned her around and took her lightly by the outstretched elbows from behind. They danced, like a pair of silent and ghostly swans, across the vast empty floor of the gallery.

He whirled and whirled, remembering steps and patterns

effortlessly, and she felt like she was flying. His magic made her steps light and her mind unburdened. He guided her with confidence, avoiding marble pillars and potted plants without breaking his step or any of the dance patterns. His touch on her elbows was light but sure. His body behind her radiated warmth, but never touched her.

It was all so proper and boring. Deep inside her, she yearned for the warmth of another person's touch and for something *not proper*. That's why she'd come out here, right? That was why she'd agreed to dance with him in the first place. If her stunt with Roald meant that she would remain a spinster for the rest of her life, would it be wrong to have a little taste of what she would miss?

Very wrong, the little voice in her mind said. It sounded like Nellie.

The music was finished, and half-hearted applause rang from the hall. Kylian let go of Johanna's elbows and warmth lingered in those small spots where he had touched her. She turned around, meeting his brown eyes.

Silence lingered between them as the magic of his touch fled her body.

"Did you like that?" he asked.

"You're a very good dancer." She felt her cheeks glowing.

He smiled.

Her heart thudded against her ribs. What was she doing? She should be sensible and go back into the garden room. Father would be looking for her in the crowd. Or King Nicholaos. And all the nobles would be wondering where she was. *Run home crying* the rumours would go.

She hesitated, but the moment to end this encounter was lost. The orchestra started the next dance, a faster piece.

"Do you want another dance?" Kylian asked.

"Not really, I'm quite hot. I should probably—" Why was she still fighting?

"Come." He took her arm.

"Where are we going?" Panic clamped around her heart. This wasn't right. Young women got into trouble this way, and everything about him smelled trouble.

That's what you wanted, right? It's your own fault, the little voice that sounded like Nellie said.

"I was on my way to the gardens. Let's get some fresh air. I'm quite keen to see this fabled gold statue that's rumoured to be here."

Johanna still protested. "I don't really know how to get there. I'm not so familiar with this part of the building. I should go back to the ball—"

If only she could think clearly, but she was hot and cold at the same time and her cheeks glowed like they were on fire.

Kylian laughed. "Oh, those people in there are boring. Were you forced to dance with the prince? Did you know he was an idiot? The king did hide his son well enough, didn't he?"

He had no right to call any member of *her* royal family an idiot, but at his words, her anger at her father re-surfaced. For all she knew, she *should* do something stupid, because . . . because she could. And she would probably be talking about this night for the rest of her life, so she might as well make sure that something good happened. Or at least something daring and not-boring.

CHAPTER 11

A SET OF DOORS at the end of the hallway led to the garden side of the palace. Bathed in moonlight, the paving looked grey save where potted plants cast ink-black shadows.

Kylian tested the doors. They opened, letting a chill breeze into the somewhat stuffy gallery. The curtains billowed inward.

She clamped her arms around herself. "Brrr."

He slipped his jerkin off his shoulders and draped it over hers. It was leather: heavy and rough and imbued with smells of forest, wood fires and something unmistakably *male* that made her shiver.

They walked onto the forecourt, where the moonlight cast deep shadows of the walls and clipped bushes. Water burbled in a crystal-clear pond. Three young willow trees lined the water, the type from the south that trailed their branches in the water.

"It's pretty," he said, pushing away the curtain of willow branches.

"Yes. I guess it's very different where you come from." She was babbling and she knew it.

"Very different," he said. "We don't have large cities, only small towns by the river, surrounded by wooded hills. This land around here is so flat. Do you know what hills look like?"

"I've seen them when going up the river with Father." Although she hadn't gone east into the Rede River, but continued to follow the Saar River to Lurezia. She'd seen *forest*, too, dense stands of trees much larger than any tree that grew in Saarland. The ground underneath was covered in leaves and moss and her footsteps had made not a sound. It was kind of scary not being able to see far or being in such a dim and dark place where evil could jump on her from behind every tree trunk.

He continued, "The forest is magic. It speaks to me of the things it has seen. It breathes life. Do you ever feel like that?"

She nodded, still hearing the whisperings in the forest when the wind raked its fingers through the boughs. There was a smell of mushrooms and rich soil and magic.

"Did you find the forest scary?" His eyes were dark in the low light, and his red hair looked black. When had he come close enough for the male scent of his body to become so overwhelming?

"I did." A bit later, she added, in a whisper, "Are there wolves where you live? Bears? Demons?"

"All of those, and more. Ghosts, wraiths, spirits. Magical creatures. Some good, some evil. People don't belong in the forest. We're mere guests and live by the rules of the forest." He sounded almost reverent. His magic was sure to involve forest and trees.

"Sounds scary."

"It's not, when you know how to listen, which I'm sure you can."

There was no point in denying her magic. "I speak to willows. The wood tells me stories."

His face split into a smile that made his eyes twinkle. "I know. Why else would I single out you, of all girls?"

Had he done that? With just a single exchanged look across a crowded hall?

"It must be quite hard, feeling magic and listening to the Shepherd denouncing all magic as evil."

"It is hard. But I want to convince the Church that magic can be used for good as well as evil."

"Bah, good luck with that. You might as well talk to a rock. They will not listen."

Normally, Johanna would have argued, but after having talked to the Shepherd about Loesie, she resigned herself to the fact that he was right.

The Church wouldn't listen. The Church had its own agenda, and that involved banishing everything they didn't understand or couldn't control. It involved getting money from the royal family that they should be spending elsewhere, or worse, didn't have.

Worse than that even, King Nicholaos was blind to what was happening.

They walked in silence, side by side. He was close enough that she could feel the warmth radiating from his body, a comforting cocoon in the chill of the night.

Via the beautifully paved and maintained path, they came to the far end of the gardens. The king had ordered a grassy mound to be built here, from where you could see over the city. Stone steps led to the top, where there was a circular paved area surrounded by a knee-high wall. The stars were out and light from the moon cast a silvery sheen over the roofs of Saardam.

"Do you know why the Moon has a ring around it?" he asked.

"Because there is mist up there where the Moon is."

He laughed. "Not quite. The Moon is so far from us that you could put the Saar and Rede rivers end to end and straight up in the sky and it wouldn't reach the Moon."

"How do you know that?"

"I study the skies."

"Do you have a looking glass? I've got one, too."

"We have the best looking glasses available in all of the western lands. My father has also hired a man called Rinius who studies the skies."

"The one who wrote the book?"

"You are familiar with it?"

"I have a copy." Father had bought it for her on his travels, knowing her interest in such things. It showed the diagrams of the stars and where planets would be at certain times of the year.

"You better hide that from your priests. Rinius is a wanted man for spreading heresy throughout all the southern lands where the Church has a hold on ruling families."

"The Church of the Triune is not the same as those southern churches."

"Tell me honestly that your priests won't declare the natural sciences heresy and I'll believe you."

Johanna said nothing. She couldn't say anything of the sort. What was more, she believed him. The sciences said many things that were against belief. To some, magic was just another science.

They continued down the mound and came to the end of the laneway, where the longitudinal flower beds gave way to features set in a circular pattern, depicting a rose.

In the middle was a pond in which stood a pedestal and on it the gilded statue of the Triune, silhouetted against the night sky.

"Urgh," Kylian said, looking up at it. "What a hideous thing."

"Are you always this rude when visiting strangers?" Not just rude, blasphemous. She had never heard anyone talk like this, not even Father's merchant friends, none of whom had any love for the Church.

"It *is* a hideous thing. Look at the slobbering mouth of the dog, and look at the hollow face. The bearded man looks like a sanctimonious piece of shit. He doesn't care about the world at all. He just cares about being *seen* to do good."

"The statue embodies the fragmented nature of the human spirit. There are three parts. Some of human nature is good, some is indifferent and shackled in tradition, and some is just plain bad."

He chuckled. "Like magic, huh?"

Unease creeping up in her, Johanna looked out over the harbour, where the boats bobbed on their moorings.

A breeze stroked her skin and brought the sound of barking dogs. Seriously, they weren't still carrying on about Master Hendricksen's monkey, were they?

"Your Church says there is no magic and any who say otherwise are evil. Your king does not believe in it."

Not just the Church—the majority of people in Saardam who didn't have magic didn't believe in the few who did. In the past, they had called people with magic witches and drowned them to test it. If a woman floated, she was a witch and would be killed. If she sank, she was not a witch, but she was dead anyway. But that had been in the time of Johanna's grandmother, and no one in the family had magic then. And there had been no Church.

Kylian continued, "Why let yourself be ruled by this Church? They are nothing but tyrants in disguise. Even the name says it all: shepherds. They expect their followers to be sheep, incapable of thinking for themselves. The Church is run by old men who are scared of magic, or maybe jealous of the ones who have it."

"They are still our people, our citizens. I do not want to be an enemy of the Church. The Church does a lot of good."

He snorted. "Some good."

"It does! It helps poor people. It gives them food and clothes."

"In exchange for their vows and adoption of their ludicrous beliefs."

Johanna glared at him. "Are you determined to offend everyone? Or are you so absorbed in your own wealth that you have no idea what it's like to be poor?"

"And you, of course, would have an excellent idea what it's like to be poor." His voice sounded sarcastic.

"I've never been poor, but I talk to people who are. If it wasn't for the Church many of them would die in winter."

"That has nothing to do with the way they treat people with magic. Poverty is a solvable, petty issue. Magic is mysterious, dangerous and it won't let itself be denied. If you ignore it, it grows stronger. You cannot banish magic, you must use it." He trailed a finger through the air, describing a path that traced the profile of her face, but his finger never touched her.

Johanna shivered. He put in words what she had thought many times.

"In Gelre, we use magic in government, and at court. We could use you. All of you with magic. If those men of the Church become too much of a problem, you will be welcome with us."

"Is this why you're here? To 'rescue' people like me from the Church?"

He chuckled. "We're here because we do not want our allies to fall to an institution that goes back to burning and drowning witches."

Which didn't answer her question. She wanted to ask him if he thought that persecution of shepherds, as happened in many eastern countries, was any better than persecution of witches, but it didn't seem so important now. Persecuted in many lands, the Church of the Triune had found fertile ground in Saardam because Shepherd Romulus offered the king solace after the tragedy of Princess Celine's death. A melting pot of people and cultures of the Western Lands, Saardam lacked a clear moral direction. The Church of the Triune fitted in that gap. That was all there was to it.

She walked around the pond so that she faced the head of the Holy God. What had he said again? *A sanctimonious piece of shit?* How dare he talk like that about people's deep beliefs?

The subtle sounds of the night drifted on the air: the soft slap of water against the quay wall on the other side of the wall around the garden, the faint sound of music, talk and laughter that came from the palace at their back. The neighing of a horse in the palace forecourt where all the noblemen's horses waited until the party had finished and they could take their masters back home again.

Kylian said softly, "You know you're not like any woman I've ever met?"

Johanna turned her head sharply to him. "Then you haven't met any real women, only dishrags."

He laughed, and it served to make her even more annoyed. "I travel all over the western lands and have not met a woman who is both pretty and in possession of magic skills. You're so wild and untamed, I can feel the magic flow. I could teach you to use your magic properly. Then nothing you ever wanted would be out of your reach."

"No, I don't want that. That's manipulating people. That's how magic gets a bad name."

"You're such a fierce one"

"When people annoy me enough."

"I annoy you?"

"Yes. When you say things like that, and when you're rude about our beliefs. What do you even know about—"

She started to walk away. This man was an insufferable arrogant prick. But she didn't get far.

"Wait." He grabbed her wrist.

"What? You want to apologise?" She tried to yank her arm out of his grip but he was very strong. "Go ahead. I'm waiting."

He paused, facing her. Dark, brooding, his gaze intense. An envelope of air around him breathed his male scent. For a while, the only sound was that of his breathing. A breeze picked up and blew a strand of his hair forward over his shoulder. The tips of it tickled on the bare skin of her upper chest.

She pulled at her arm again. "If you're so honourable, you would let me go. My father will come looking for me any time now."

His face showed mock surprise. "Oh? I thought you would be too mature for these sorts of tricks. But you can always become like one of those dumb ladies inside." He put on a high voice. "Let me go or I'm going to scream."

"I can scream if you want me to."

"Be my guest. Scream."

He took a step back, while still holding on to her arm.

There was no way she was going to give him that satisfaction. She tried to twist out of his grip. Her voice came out as a grunt. "Let me go."

She twisted her arm further, sure she'd have bruises tomorrow. But the only effect of her struggle was that she came closer to him and his grip tightened. He laughed.

"You're doing that all wrong. You have to hold my wrist, like so."

His other hand took hold of her free hand and placed it on the arm that held hers.

"Grab it tight so that I can't move."

She did, although she had no illusion that he could still move as much as he wanted.

"Now twist sharply."

She did as he said and her arm came free.

"See, that was easy."

"You let me go."

"If you do this quickly, it will take most people by surprise. Remember it for when an unwanted suitor tries to grab you. Want to try again?"

Johanna hesitated. This was one strange man. Dangerous, challenging, mysterious, crackling with magic.

She faced him, her chest heaving with deep breaths from the struggle. He returned her stare, unwavering and not in the least flustered.

Johanna's cheeks felt like they were on fire.

He said, his voice low, "Has a man ever kissed those ruby lips of yours?"

"What business is that of yours?"

"It's more interesting for me if it's the first time for you."

"Who said you could kiss me?"

He laughed, trailing his finger over her cheek. His touch made her shiver. "Twenty-three and never been kissed?"

"Twenty-four." She looked defiantly into his eyes. He was talking to her as if she were a little girl, thinking she was afraid of men, huh?

"See, I'm not holding you against your will." He spread his hands. "You can run to your father if you want. Run, little girl, run!"

Johanna didn't move.

Kylian leaned closer, enveloping her in his warmth. His

lips brushed hers fleetingly. He smelled of leather, smoke and fire.

"Like that?" He was teasing her.

"That's fine by me," she whispered. "I'm not afraid of you."

"Well, there's plenty of time to establish the truth of that."

He took her in a rough grip and pressed his mouths on hers. His lips forced hers apart and his tongue came into her mouth. She hadn't expected that, and let out involuntary moan. She struggled to breathe. His hands slid up her sides, over the tight bodice of the dress.

He let go and stared at her in the moonlight. He chuckled. "Still not afraid?"

Johanna gasped for breath but shook her head, her heart still thudding. Was that what kissing was like? It was disgusting.

But it was naughty. It was like what men said about smoking. You hated it the first time, thought it was all right the second and after that you couldn't stop doing it.

He was still holding her waist, looking down into her face, his lips slightly parted.

That second kiss was coming up right now. He covered her mouth with his and now she knew what was coming, didn't flinch or try to pull back. She relaxed in his arms.

Yes, that was much better.

He chuckled. "My, you're learning fast." His lips brushed the tip of her nose. "You're so pretty, wasting your life in this silly provincial town. Since you're not going to marry the prince, would you like to come back with me? I could teach you magic. You could talk to Rinius, be his assistant, even. We could . . . continue this activity undisturbed." He ran his tongue along the line of her jaw.

Johanna shivered.

Get out of here, start anew, what an opportunity. She'd disappointed her father by refusing to marry Roald. She didn't want Octavio Nieland. She didn't want to marry at all, but if she had to, why not someone from outside the stifling Saardam society?

He kissed her again, this time longer. She tried replying to him, tickling his tongue with hers. He chuckled without breaking the kiss. His hands raked through her hair.

Then, suddenly, there was a sound she recognised: the ringing of church bells, the clanging distorted by the breeze.

At this time of day?

Johanna stiffened. Kylian let her go.

"What's going on?" she whispered.

He said nothing, but turned his face into the wind. His eyes were alert, his face tense.

"Can you feel anything?" She still didn't know what type of magic he had. Something to do with the forest. Maybe he had wind magic, too. Was it possible for one person to have more than one kind of magic?

She repeated, "What's going on?" Her heart was thudding.

He looked sideways, and then without a word, bolted down the path.

She called after him, "Hey!"

But he didn't listen or stop. He jumped into the hedge that shielded the garden's outer wall from view, pulled himself up over the wall and down the other side, leaving Johanna standing stunned and alone in the garden.

She clamped her hands around herself. When had the air become so cold?

Distant sounds drifted from the city: the barking and howling of dogs. The neighing of horses. People shouting.

A cat raced through the garden, yowling, with all its hair standing on end. Goodness, what possessed that animal?

Feeling shaken, Johanna climbed onto the mound where

they had looked at the stars so that she could see over the wall. There was an orange glow in the city, a street or so back from the harbour. Vicious flames rose from the roof of one of the canal houses. That was nowhere near *her* house, was it? She traced the outlay of the streets in her mind. She didn't *think* it was in her street.

There was a soft sound of footsteps behind her. Johanna turned around.

Someone had come into the garden from the gallery and now walked up the steps to where she stood. A woman, thin and shrouded in black. Her tread was light, as if she floated.

Johanna curtsied before the queen. "My excuses for being in your garden, Your Highness. I was hot and—"

"What is going on in town?" Queen Cygna's voice was sharp, almost nervous, and with the distinct accent of the northern lands. She gasped and raised a dainty hand to her mouth. "Fire."

Johanna turned around. The fire had spread. Flames licked the roof of one of the harbour-side warehouses. "Is that Master Deim's warehouse?"

The Queen couldn't answer that. She probably didn't know who Master Deim was.

"Listen to the poor horses," the queen said.

The breeze brought sounds of neighing and men shouting and dogs barking. In fact, the horses had been nervous all afternoon. There was magic in the air and she couldn't feel it.

"With your permission, Your Highness, I think we should go inside," she said, and Queen Cygna did not object. She walked silent next to Johanna on the path towards the palace. There were things Johanna wanted to say, but didn't know how to broach them. About Roald, about Father, about herself. But she couldn't find the right words. The queen had seemed so very fragile and upset at Roald's misbehaviour. She didn't want to risk saying something inappropriate.

Just outside the door, the queen held Johanna back.

"Thank you." Her voice was soft.

"Your Highness?" *Thank you*, what for?

The queen hesitated. Seen through the black veil, her face was exquisite, her skin soft and pale, as yet marred by few lines, her eyes the clearest blue. A few wisps of flaxen hair peeped out from underneath the black lace.

"Roald is a good boy. He gets confused easily and takes instructions literally. He doesn't know when it is appropriate to say certain . . . things. He gets these ideas into his head and wants to talk about them with everyone. I'm afraid his father did some explaining about what's involved in getting married, and he took an unexpected interest to certain private parts of it. I'm truly sorry for anything upsetting that he might have said to you. But I say again, even if he is unusual, he is a good man and would never harm anyone."

"I understand, Your Highness."

"No. You do not." She patted Johanna on the arm and then froze, looking over Johanna's shoulder. "Look."

As they both watched, a creature sleek and agile like a cat, but made entirely out of fire, jumped from the flames onto another roof, setting it alight with a touch of its tail.

Queen Cygna gasped. "Fire demons." The firelight made her face look pale. Her eyes were wide.

"I need to go to my father. His warehouse is somewhere over there."

"Yes, you should do that." The queen's eyes were wide. "But after you have done that, you should get out of here, and you should warn everyone to do the same. You cannot fight these creatures and their masters."

Johanna's heart jumped. "Your Highness, do you know what those creatures are and where they come from?" She saw snarling demons shown to her by Loesie's basket. A chill went over her. The prick of magic made the air crackle.

Loesie. She was in the barn. She was either possessed and part of the evil, or she was in danger down there near the fire.

The queen said in a low voice, "My husband and his advisors played with things they didn't understand. The Burovian priests were blind for money, and promised things that were not theirs to promise. My husband gave them money, even though I told him it was a bad idea, but like so many times, the voice of a woman doesn't count. He didn't listen. He was too keen to have Celine back, and he believed that they could resurrect her."

"He was talking to a necromancer?"

The queen nodded, her face sad. "Whether or not he could do as his disciples said remains to be seen. I don't think so, but he's a powerful magician."

"Who is this man?"

"I never saw him, and I don't think my husband did either. We dealt with his followers. They call themselves the dawn order, but they're nothing more than practitioners of dark magic. I told him not to get involved, but he was too impatient."

"Are these priests from the sanatorium where Roald was?"

"No, no, not at all. Those good men have also come into danger because of this ill-considered deal. They're also angry with us, with good reason. The order of the dawn has performed evil rituals in the forest that have disturbed the demons. It was my hope that our withdrawal of Roald could stop their anger, but it's already too late. Humans and magical creatures both come under the influence of anger. Only humans are capable of forgiveness. You must run and save yourself while you still can. All of us are lost already. Wherever we go, they will find us. Don't trust any easterners."

And then, silently and much more quickly than Johanna would have expected for a royal, she was gone.

CHAPTER 12

JOHANNA'S HEART still beat high in her throat when she came back into the main hall, where the festivities continued as if nothing had happened. The air was heavy with the smell of sweat and alcohol. Waltzing couples filled the dance floor. The music, talk and laughter drowned out the shouts and neighs from outside. The doors on the far side of the hall were closed, so none of the stewards had yet come in to warn their masters and no one had seen the fire.

Don't trust any easterners. There were easterners everywhere in the crowd, amongst the guests and the servants, and in the distinguished party at the dais. There was no way that they were all bad, and there was no way to determine if any of them had knowledge of what was happening outside.

The king sat alone at the dais, flanked by two empty chairs. Why didn't Queen Cygna warn her husband about the fire?

Father sat on the other side of the hall, talking to Master Deim. He didn't look like he'd missed her, but she was sure he had. She felt guilty and horrible all in one. It was not good for business to let feelings rule your actions, Father would often say, and she had well and truly done that. However, there were more urgent issues to deal with now.

Johanna pushed herself across the dance floor. "Excuse me, excuse me. Please let me through."

That earned her a few turned heads and surprised expressions. One nobleman said something lewd about the prince, but fortunately he was too drunk for his words to make sense.

Johanna was about halfway when the doors to the hall burst open and a couple of palace guards ran in. The panicked neighs of horses drifted into the hall through the doors which the guards had left open. People stopped dancing. The orchestra played on, but several of the musicians were looking at the open door instead of the conductor. A couple of noblemen ran into the foyer.

One of the guards was talking to the king, who nodded. His face looked pale and old. He dismissed the guard with a wave of his hand and rose.

The music stopped. Now even the last couples stopped dancing. Some people made complaining noises, others wondered aloud about the time.

"Friends, family," the king said. Even his voice sounded tired. "It seems like it is time to end the festivities. Please go home and be safe."

Two guards accompanied him down the steps.

People around Johanna protested.

"What? It's too early."

"What's going on?"

The king said no more. He made his way through the hall surrounded by the royal guards to fend off the questions.

Johanna felt revolted. How had the country ended up with such a weak man for a king?

He was not going to tell the people of the predicament he was in? He was not going to warn them about what he'd done or apologise? Pray for their safety? Even tell them that the city was on fire?

The orchestra members were packing their instruments and the first people were already leaving the hall.

She'd better go and find Father.

But now that everyone was agitated and looking around for their friends and family, she couldn't see him anywhere. Not in the hall and not in the entrance foyer, where courtiers were playing business as usual, handing the noble lords and ladies back their coats and cloaks. A line of people filed out of the entrance. A concerned murmur filled the space where previously there had been music and merrymaking.

Johanna pushed through the crowd, looking for Father's blue coat. She called him and asked people if they'd seen him. No one had.

Then a man on the front porch yelled, "There!"

A woman shouted, "Oh, look! Is that near our house?"

Another woman shrieked.

Several people started yelling at once.

"What is that thing?"

"It's a work of evil magic."

Johanna was in the back of the crowd and could only see the orange glow of the fire against the pillars of the entrance porch, but she'd seen the fire devil.

There was a commotion outside, voices shouting, horses neighing, the crack of whips.

A gust of wind brought a wave of heat from across from the city. It filled the foyer and blew open all doors in the entrance hall. Curtains billowed; the candles blew out. A scent of fire wafted on the wind. People around Johanna pushed and screamed. The wind pricked with magic.

Several people turned around and ran back towards the palace, but the palace guards were just shutting the doors and wouldn't let anyone in.

One guard called, "Everyone go home, go home now!"

Outside on the steps, groups of nobles were still waiting for their coaches to turn up. A long line of them filed out the gate. The horses were nervous and several grooms had trouble keeping their charges under control.

The animals could smell magic. They had been smelling magic all day.

Johanna walked up and down the stairs, yelling for Father, but she didn't see him and no one knew where he was. She couldn't imagine that Father would have gone home without her. Where was he? Father was the only family she had left. Panic clamped around her heart.

She ran up and down the stairs along the line of people waiting to be picked up by coaches.

All the nobles were agitated, looking around for family, craning their necks to see if their coaches had arrived yet. She spotted Julianna Nieland, crying on the shoulder of her brother. At least they were together. Other nobles, too, were in panic, wondering aloud about the safety of their houses. Older people talked about legendary fires of the past, most of which had resulted in significant damage to large parts of town. That did nothing to ease people's minds.

Some people were too nervous to keep waiting and walked out the gate. The church bells were still ringing. Horses neighed and their handlers shouted. Over the top of all that noise came the occasional pop of flames.

Father had to have been left behind inside the palace. That was the only conclusion Johanna could reach. Maybe if she asked the guards, they would open the door for her.

The moment she decided to go back, there was a tremendous crash, followed by a growl, and splintering of wood. One of the solid palace doors had burst open in a jagged hole of splinters. Metal flashed in the darkness underneath the porch. A guard shouted, his voice suddenly cut off in a snarl.

A woman screamed. Several dark shapes came out of the wrecked door and bounded into the forecourt. They were soft-footed and agile like cats, but much bigger.

People were pushing back up the stairs. Johanna was in the middle of the mad crowd, barely able to see where the steps were. She stumbled several times, each time afraid that she would fall and that the crowd would trample her.

A young woman fell and couldn't get up because other people were stepping on her dress. Nobody seemed to care. Johanna tried to reach out to the woman, but her arm wasn't long enough and the crowd swept her away.

A horse in the forecourt reared, kicking its front legs. The coach behind it tipped on its side. The cabin splintered. Several of the dark creatures ran to it. One grabbed the horse by the throat. There was a woman's high-pitched scream—cut off. A snarl.

"Oh, by the Holy Triune," a man called out.

It was surely a sign of despair that *nobles* were invoking the Triune.

Johanna gathered the folds of her dress around her, but the awkward hoops made it hard to move. She couldn't see her feet. Couldn't see where the steps were. People pushed her in all directions. Some were trying to get down, others, like her, wanted to get up. There was screaming. There were snarls. Harsh voices of men in a foreign language in the forecourt.

Johanna reached the porch, ran between the marble columns and stepped through the wrecked door. The bottom of her dress caught. The wind had blown out all the lights in the foyer. Snarls and growls and screams continued behind her.

She ran across the foyer with its floor covered with glass and splintered wood, into the big hall where it was dark but where mere moments before everyone had been dancing and laughing. She went out the side door into the garden room, dark, too, with a lingering scent of perfume where Queen Cygna had been. A sharp breeze cut in through the open doors on the far side of the hall. The glass lay in shards on the ground. Someone ran in, carrying a sword. He stopped.

"No! Go back!" His voice was rough with fear.

Johanna pressed herself against the wall in an alcove. She didn't *think* his shout was directed at her.

Several figures ran into the gallery from behind her, over Princess Celine's gravestone. Three—four men with long spears. With them was a dark, round-backed and long-haired creature that broke into a flat-footed run. It spotted the guard and grabbed him around the throat before he could run. He screamed as he fell, and the animal snarled, shaking its head vigorously so that the dead man's legs flopped from one side to the other like a rag doll.

One of the bandits whistled hard. The creature lifted its head and loped back to its owners. It halted in a rectangle of moonlight that fell into the gallery through a window. It had small, furry ears, little beady eyes, and a long nose that wriggled as the animal turned its head and looked from side to side. A bear.

It passed not a few steps from where she hid. She pressed herself into the alcove as much as she could. The door to the main hall was at her back and it could open at any time. Worse, the wood showed her what was happening on the other side of the door.

A couple of citizens had entered the hall. Silhouetted against the glare from the fires outside, she counted two men in uniform and a group of five or six nobles, judging by the clothing. A woman in the group was crying, holding her companion, a man in a ruffled shirt. Another group followed them, these ones running from whatever pursued them outside.

A second bear bounded into the entrance, followed by two tall men in furs with long hair.

"It's following us!" one of the women screamed.

A men yelled, "Be gone with you, demon!"

But the bear jumped for his throat with a snarl. The man's shout turned into a scream. While the two bears rounded up the nobles in the far corner, the bandits who had walked past Johanna had entered the hall where they met up with their comrades with claps on shoulders. One of the men whistled.

As one, the two bears leapt into the group of nobles.

Johanna hardly dared breathe.

People tried to run, but the women wore stupid dresses that were not suited to running. The men were unarmed, had never held a weapon and had no idea how to defend themselves. None had any magic, except Johanna, and she had no idea how to use it to help them. She couldn't stand it any longer; she had to step away from the door.

In the chaos of the garden room, the panicked shouts became screams of terror, mixed with unearthly snarls. Something fell with a thud across the open doors into the hall, a few steps away from her. It was one of the nobles, dressed in court finery. The side of his head hit the ground hard. He twitched and didn't move. A dark stain spread out from under him.

Johanna pressed herself against the wall, careful not to touch the wood. She didn't dare run towards the garden. Once she was there, she was trapped because with this dress she couldn't even begin to try climbing the walls as Kylian had done. But the bandits would discover her soon.

The screams became less and trailed off altogether. The only sounds now were the foreign voices, and the snorts and sniffles of the bears.

Those voices became, too, became softer, as if the bandits were walking out of the other side of the hall. Johanna pressed her hand to the wood once more, just in time to see the silhouettes of bandits and the bears in the doorway as they walked into the foyer.

What now?

Johanna sneaked to the door and looked around the corner.

A single torch still burned in the hall close to the door. She stepped carefully around the body of the nobleman and slipped the light out of its bracket.

Holding it aloft, she slowly turned around. The floor of the hall was covered in bodies, noblemen in their finery with bloodstains spreading on their white shirts, noble ladies with their dresses ripped.

A wave of dizziness overcame her.

Father. She desperately didn't want to look at the dead, but took her torch to each body on the floor. All those fine clothes covered in blood. Several victims had their faces ripped off.

Father was not there.

Dazed as if in a bad dream, she went into the entrance hall, where she found the bodies of five guards in puddles of blood. No one left alive there either.

The palace steps were empty, orange in the glow of the fire.

In a corridor off the hall, she found another body in brown robes. One of the Shepherd's helpers. Her head reeled with the idiocy of it all. Who in their right minds would kill a harmless priest?

But a chill took hold of her. Priests were probably what the attackers had been after.

The door to a room on the right stood open. Johanna went inside. Her footfalls were soft on luxurious carpet. This appeared to be an audience room of some sort, with a number of chairs around a low table.

Even before she saw them, Johanna knew by the tang of blood that there were dead people in this room. Part of her wanted to run away. She had seen enough blood to last her a lifetime, but part of her had to know who the victims were.

On the couch, a red stain spread out from the body of a woman in a long black gown with lace. Queen Cygna's veil had fallen off, and her open-eyed face looked surprised. There was a second body on the carpet. Johanna didn't need to see the Carmine cloak to recognise the king.

She brought her hand to her mouth to stop herself crying out. Her head was reeling. What had King Nicholaos done to justify this carnage?

Worse, somewhere in the palace, the men were still on their rampage. They would find Roald. He would not be able to defend himself.

Saarland was finished. Everything was lost.

CHAPTER 13

SURPRISINGLY, Johanna's head remained clear enough to think.

First, the crown and staff were symbols of the Carmine House, and no bandits should get their hands on them. She dropped to her knees to fish the crown out from under the table. The staff, though, was under the king's body. Carefully, she rolled the king over. She had to do her best not to focus on the gaping wound in his stomach or she would surely faint, or throw up, or both. His face was undamaged, with his eyes half open. Carefully, she unfolded his fingers, still warm, and removed the staff. She took it and the crown into the corridor. A few doors down was a broom cupboard. Johanna stumbled in, upsetting a bucket with the bottom of her dress, and placed the precious items on the top shelf. She pushed the door shut. There. At least the bandits would have to look for the symbols of Carmine power.

Next, she had to get out and save herself and Father and the house. Then they would take the *Lady Sara* upriver and go to Mother's family.

It felt improper to walk away from the King and Queen,

who could have been her parents-in-law, but she could do nothing except whisper a few lines of prayer. King Nicholaos would have liked that.

The hallway was still empty. As fast as she dared without making too much noise, Johanna ran out the door. The steps were awkward because she couldn't see her feet in that stupid dress. Then through to the forecourt, now a mess of ruined coaches, dead horses, bodies and fine clothes covered in blood. Already, flames licked the top of the palace roof.

She stopped briefly at each body, but saw none that looked like Father.

A man with a bear stood at the gate. It gave a low grunt, probably because it smelled Johanna. The man said something and the animal settled.

Johanna slipped out of a side gate.

First she had to go home to get changed out of this ridiculous dress.

She ran through the streets of the merchant district. Many people ran through the streets, some carrying packs and children. A coach driver was trying to control his panicked horse while a noble family got into the cab. Where would they be going? These bandits were destroying everything in sight. The sky was orange with the glow of the fire that would lay all of the inner city to ashes. This was worse than the big fires of the past.

Johanna ran. The hoops of the dress flopped awkwardly around her legs. Her shoes hurt. She wished she had her clogs.

Once she spotted a group of men with two hairy and flat-footed bears.

One pushed in a shop door with ease, before a man threw a burning torch inside the shop. Within moments, flames burst out the windows and the glass broke. The men laughed in their guttural, foreign voices.

Johanna ran.

Her house. Father, Nellie.

The houses at the far end of her street were already on fire. Against the glow, a group of people were fighting in the street. Women screamed. A dark shape lay motionless on the cobbles.

Fire reflected in the upstairs windows of Johanna's house, still untouched but probably not for long. She ran up the front steps, pushed the front door open. Her heart jumped. Would Father have made it back here?

"Nellie, Father?"

There was no reply, except the sound of breaking glass from further down the street.

"Nellie, where are you?"

Johanna walked into the kitchen—empty—the living room—empty, too. Koby would have gone home. Nellie's sewing work lay on the table in the living room, but obviously, she wasn't here either.

It was useless. There was no one here, and too little time to look for them. Johanna ran upstairs, pulling at the laces that held her bodice together. The bodice loosened, but she couldn't reach all the buttons. She pulled the bodice down, and then tried to lift it over her head, but it was no use. She pulled at the skirt with the hoops. The dress was stuck. "Nellie!"

There was no reply. She pulled again, but the fabric was too tough. She stumbled down the stairs into the kitchen. Now where did Koby keep the knives? She rummaged through the drawers, eventually finding a pair of scissors. They were old and blunt, and cutting through the fabric was hard, but she freed herself from the skirt with the hoops and then managed to wrench the buttons loose. *Sorry, Mistress Daphne.*

Then she went back up the stairs in her underclothes.

People were shouting in the street. The smell of smoke drifted under the door. She took her comfortable everyday dress from the cupboard and slipped it on. Then her vest over the top. Then she collected a handful of other clothes in a soft travel bag that she had used to go to Lurezia.

Then back to the kitchen, grabbed a tea towel, and yanked the handle of the pump until water came out, wet the towel and tied it over her nose and mouth. Then she grabbed Father's long coat from the stand, wet it as well, and put it on. It was freezing. Then her clogs. And her second-best shoes just to be certain. She buttoned up the bag.

She opened the front door. A cloud of acrid smoke billowed through the street. Several people ran past at high speed.

She pulled the front door shut behind her and ran down the steps, down the street the way she'd come. Fire was already eating at the neighbour's house.

Down the street, into the marketplace, past burning shops. A woman called her name. "Johanna, stop, Johanna!"

She stopped, seeing a thin figure run towards her.

"Nellie!" She swept Nellie up in her arms. She smelled clean and warm

"Oh, thank the holy spirit, Mistress Johanna, you're alive."

"Where is Father?"

"Didn't he come back with you?"

"No, I ran from the palace. I couldn't find him anywhere." A deep sense of guilt took hold of her. She should have looked better. Father would be around there somewhere looking for her. What if he was injured and needed her help?

"I was looking for you and Koby," Nellie said. Firelight reflected in her eyes. "And then I saw the fires and saw those creatures. I didn't know what to do. Those are the demons, right?"

"They're bears. They came into the palace," Johanna said. "The king is dead. The queen is dead."

Nellie clamped her hands over her mouth. "What about Prince Roald?"

"I don't know, Nellie." How many people had been killed there?

"Let's go home and wait for the master."

"We can't. There's fighting in the street. The house will burn soon. No one is even trying to put out the fire." All the houses were built mostly of wood. There would be nothing left of the city.

"No. Then where can we go?" Nellie's voice sounded small.

"I was going to the *Lady Sara*." But a sense of dread took hold of her. She had wanted to take the sloop upriver and wait out the trouble, but without anyone to handle the cows, could she even get it out of the harbour?

They ran through the streets. Every time Johanna saw the silhouette of a man, she hoped it was Father. Maybe he would have gone to the harbour as well. Several times, they had to hide away from bands of men with bears.

There was fighting at the quayside as well, and men were breaking windows of merchant offices. A fire burned in a warehouse, and its reflection of the flames in the water was gold.

Father's office was still safe, but a fight blocked Johanna and Nellie's way to it.

The fire in the Deim warehouse had spread to neighbouring warehouses.

"Look at that, Nellie. It's getting so close to the armoury." If that caught fire, there would be disaster.

The ships' boys had moved the *Lady Sara* to the dock at Father's barn, which was still free of fire, but she and Nellie couldn't get there because the warehouses along the wharf were on fire.

Nellie froze. The firelight reflected in her eyes. She raised her hands to her mouth. "It's terrible. What can we do? Where can we go?"

"Come with me."

Johanna ran to the quay. The low tide had uncovered a set of barnacle-covered slippery steps that ran down to the water. Between the larger boats lay a dingy with a pair of oars. Johanna jumped in, starting to untie the knot.

"Come, quickly. Be careful, though, it's—"

Nellie gave a little yell and slipped, falling in a heap on the steps.

Johanna jumped out, almost slipped herself on the algae on the steps.

"Are you all right?"

Several men yelled on the quay above them. There was the sound of running footsteps. Johanna threw Father's dark cloak over herself and Nellie and crouched on the steps. The men ran past.

The roof of the armoury was now on fire. "Quick, Nellie." She more or less dragged Nellie into the boat.

Then she untied the rope and grabbed the oars. Her first stroke missed the water and the right oar clanged into the hull of the large boat.

She pushed the oars deeper. They now found resistance and slowly, the dinghy moved into open water. Oof, it was a long time since she'd done this.

As they pulled away from the quay, the glow of fire became stronger. The entire row of offices on the quay were on fire. A couple of men ran across with buckets. Johanna wasn't sure where they were going or what they hoped to do.

Nellie was crying. "Oh, what can we do, what can we do?"

"Be quiet, that's what. We don't want to draw attention to ourselves."

They reached the sea cow barn and went in under the ship doors. The animals were restless, sloshing in the water, blowing and snorting. They weren't crazy—they could feel that something was up.

Several bumped the dinghy, increasing Nellie's panic even further.

There was a rustle in the corner of the barn, amongst the stack of crates.

Johanna called, "Loesie? Loesie, are you there?"

A couple of crates moved aside, and Loesie rose, her eyes wide in the glow of the fires. "Ghghghgh!" Her eyes were wide. She pointed to the door, where fire was reflected in the water.

"Yes, the whole city is on fire. They were demons, as you said. The royal family has meddled with evil magic and now the demons are angry." Oh, why had Master Willems said nothing about it earlier? Most of the merchants knew of his hidden talent. They would have believed him, even if they'd never say so in public. They would have started rumours and people would have been warned.

And now . . . the entire sky glowed orange with fire in the direction of the palace. There was shouting and screaming. Glass shattered. Things exploded in the warehouses.

"We have to get out, before they discover us," Johanna said. *Before the armoury goes up.*

"But how?" Nellie sounded close to tears.

"We'll take the *Lady Sara*."

"But you don't know anything about sloops."

"I know a bit." Not much, and she'd only seen the deckhands do things. She had no doubt that getting the cows harnessed and going in the same direction seemed easier than it was.

"Ghghghghgh," Loesie said, pointing at her chest.

"Loesie knows about sloops," Johanna said. "She's come here by herself." Although the barge owned by Loesie's family was much smaller than the *Lady Sara*.

Nellie edged further away from Loesie.

Loesie was already wriggling the harness rigging off the hooks, and filling the feed pouches with carrots, like Johanna had seen her father's boatsmen do many times. The cows splashed and snorted in the water, raising their rounded and whiskered snouts; they wanted the carrots. More than anything else, they wanted to get out of here. But even over the noise they made, there was the sound of shouting at the quay.

Johanna opened the barn door a fraction.

Down the wharf, a group of bandits attacked a group of men. There was shouting, swords were drawn. Several of the men looked like palace guards. The others were rogues with long hair and leather jerkins. They had dogs, and a shaggy bear that ran across the quay. It disturbed her how well those large creatures obeyed people. She'd heard about bear magic, but what was the power of bear magic? Why couldn't she feel it?

One, then two people fell onto the cobbles and didn't get up.

Johanna felt chilled watching. These bandits just mowed innocent people down as if they were animals. Whatever the royal family had done, this didn't justify it.

Loesie had walked down the platform to the water and had hooked the rigging onto the sea cows' harnesses. Six animals were already chomping on carrots; a couple of big hairy bodies were jostling for the remaining two spots.

"Come, Nellie, help me." Johanna grabbed the corner of a bag of carrots. It was much too heavy for her alone to lift. Nellie grabbed the other corner. Together, they heaved it out of the barn, onto the jetty and the gangplank, onto the flatly sloping cargo hatch of the *Lady Sara*.

They carried a number of other sacks to the deck. There were potatoes, firewood, oiled cloth, and crates of which Johanna had no idea what they contained, but it would be something useful, because things needed for the boats were stored in here. Freight went into the warehouse.

"Take as much as you can," she said to Nellie when passing her on the way out.

Nellie was crying; the front of her apron was filthy. "Oh, Mistress Johanna, I don't think I can lift any more. My arms are so sore. What are we going to do?"

"We'll stay alive, that's what we'll do. We have to get out of here before they discover us. We can come back later, when the fires are out and the demons have had enough of setting fire to things." *Or until there is nothing left to burn.* Johanna's arms were sore, too, but she wasn't going to say anything about that.

"But where can we go?" Nellie's eyes were wide.

Fire lit up the sky in a terrible display of orange. The palace guards were still fighting on the quay in front of Father's office. The building itself was on fire. More and more bandits ran onto the quay, and the poor guards were heavily outnumbered. Any moment and the bandits would start setting fire to the boats.

Loesie walked along the side of the *Lady Sara*, holding the reins. A tricky operation. If the cows panicked and bolted, she would go over the edge or let go of the reins. Many an inexperienced boatsman had spent hours waiting for escaped clutches of cows to return after such a mishap.

Johanna heaved a couple more bags on board. She helped Nellie with a stack of oiled cloth.

The roof of the armoury was on fire and it would be a

matter of time before something exploded. The cows would panic. This was their only chance to get out.

Then there was a heavy splash: someone had fallen into the water.

Johanna gasped and turned around, but Loesie still stood on the deck.

"Look, there!" Nellie sat on the cover to the cargo hold, pointing.

On the other side of the harbour, a bandit peered into the darkness of the water, bow drawn. He didn't fire. Possibly he couldn't see the head of the man swimming. But backlit against the fires at the quay, Johanna could.

"Who is it?" Nellie asked.

"I don't know. One of the ships' boys or fishermen, probably. Let's go."

"But he'll drown."

"Looks like he swims very well." Surprisingly well, actually. "He'll save himself. Is everyone ready?"

Loesie had the rigging tied up securely. The sea cows were pulling at their harness. Johanna jumped onto the jetty and loosened the ropes. The *Lady Sara* slowly receded from the quay.

"Ghghghgh!" Loesie stood at the stern. She had tied up the reins to the bar across the deck for that purpose. She pointed at the water.

The swimmer was coming in their direction. A weak man's voice sounded over the water. "Stop . . . stop . . . don't leave without me."

What to do? What if he was one of the rogues? No, that couldn't be.

"Loesie, wait. We'll pick him up. Nellie, come on. Stop crying. Help me with this rope." The trailing end of the rope had fallen into the water. Johanna pulled it to the harbour-side of the boat, and tried to throw it at the man. But the rope was heavy with salty water. The rough fibre scratched her hands. When she threw it, she almost toppled into the water after it.

The rope made a splash in the water. It fell far short of the swimmer.

In her mind, she heard Adrian's laughter. *It will be a long time before you make a decent deckhand, mistress.* He'd said that so many times after she'd fumbled trying to "help" him. Then again, she had never considered that one day she would have to be a real deckhand.

To her surprise, the end of the rope hadn't disappeared under water: there was a wooden float on the end.

The swimmer had come closer. She whispered as loudly as she dared, "Here, hang onto the end of the rope!"

Moments later he grabbed the float. Johanna hauled at the rope, but couldn't lift him out of the water.

"Use the handholds!" she yelled down, but either he didn't hear it or he couldn't see them. "Nellie, Loesie, help me!"

It took all three of them, or mostly Loesie and Johanna, to pull the man up on the deck. He fell to his hands and knees, coughing. He wore a dark jacket of velvet that would have been very heavy in the water judging by the size of the puddle that formed around him. His trousers had ripped and were covered in mud.

"C . . . cold." His teeth chattered.

Despite the state of his clothes, he didn't look like a common citizen. In fact, he looked like he had been a guest at the ball.

There were shouts from the quay. A group of huge men with long hair and leather jerkins ran across, pursuing a couple of palace guards who ran onto the wharf where the *Lady Sara* had been moored.

"Let's go!" Johanna yelled at Loesie. "Go, go, go! Come on, help me get him into the cabin." This to Nellie.

Nellie came and grabbed the man's other arm. He went into another coughing spasm.

"Killed, they're all killed," he whispered. He was shivering.

Johanna pulled him to his feet and together with Nellie, moved across the narrow walkway between the sloping lids on the cargo hold and the railing. Meanwhile Loesie yanked at the reins. The sea cows threshed in the harness; they wanted to be out of here. Slowly, the boat started moving again.

A group of men with two bears ran onto the quay. One threw a burning torch which trailed sparks as it flew through the air. It landed on the deck, but Johanna could kick it off the other side before it had ignited anything. The flames hissed out into the water and probably spooked the sea cows, but fortunately, that made them move more quickly.

Soon, the *Lady Sara* was too far away from the wharf to be within their reach. Shouts drifted over the water and echoed in the stillness. They sounded like curses, but in what language she didn't know.

Then—a brief moment of eerie calm, followed by a huge roar of fire. The very air was alive with vibration. Next, the roof of the armoury blew sky high. The sound wave followed moments later, and a blast of hot air. Burning debris rained over the surrounding quay. A ball of fire billowed out, devouring everything in its path. Every boat within reach of the fireball was set alight, right down to the steps where Johanna and Nellie had taken the dinghy.

Nellie and Johanna finally reached the cabin with their charge. The door was narrow and it took some manoeuvring to get the man inside, unsteady on his feet as he was.

Once inside, Johanna sat him on the chair at Father's writing desk while she searched for blankets or any spare men's clothes that Father or the deckhands might have stored here.

The cabin's main windows faced away from the glow of the inferno. While moonlight shone into the side window, it was pitch dark in the far corners of the cabin. There was a storm light against the back wall, but while there was probably a candle in it, she had no way to light it. Tomorrow, she would have to get out the flint and steel and get the galley fire going, but for now, they would have to survive in the dark. She hoped there would be wood or peat on board. Stupid that she hadn't checked. It would be miserable on board without a fire.

Their refugee's teeth chattered.

Johanna found a blanket on a shelf and handed it to him. "Here, take off your wet clothes and use this blanket."

He rose from the chair and held his arms wide. "Can you . . . can you help me?" He shivered so much that he could barely speak.

For one moment Johanna considered that undressing a man would be seen as highly inappropriate, but then she decided to hell with it. He was wet, cold, exhausted. They were all tired and should help each other.

With hands numb through fatigue and cold, she tackled his sodden jacket—oh boy, that thing was heavy. She gave it to Nellie to find a place to hang it to dry. Nellie disappeared into the door at the back that led to the galley.

Then the shirt. She peeled it off his thin arms.

Through the window at the front of the cabin, she could see Loesie in the moonlight, standing at the stern watching the cows.

The *Lady Sara* made a slight turn. Moonlight came into the window and showed her the man's face.

It was Prince Roald.

CHAPTER 14

JOHANNA STARED at Prince Roald, not knowing what to say. All she could think of was the way he had stared at her chest during the ball, which now seemed ages ago.

Behind her Nellie gasped. "Mistress Johanna, what are you doing?"

A soft glow spread through the cabin. Nellie stood the door opening carrying a storm light. Bless the *Lady Sara*'s crew. Someone had left coals burning in a firebox.

Johanna would have laughed had this been a normal day. With her taking off Roald's shirt, this could be seen in an entirely different way. But it was not a normal day, and he was shivering and his clothes soaking wet. Did Nellie ever stop worrying about what was appropriate?

Also, she obviously didn't recognise him. With the way in which his parents had kept him hidden, how many people would know what the prince looked like?

Johanna handed Nellie the wet shirt. "Here, hang that out, too." She was starting to shiver as well, and hoped that there would be more blankets.

Roald gave a sob. His face twisted into a pained mask. "They're all gone," he cried. "All gone, all gone!" He spread his hands. His palms were scratched from where he had cut himself clambering up the rope.

"I know." Johanna draped the blanket over his shoulders. If he was a normal person, she might have hugged him, but now she didn't know if it would make him angry. Or, heaven forbid, if it would make him stare at her breasts again. He was much stronger than she was and if he got something in his mind, she didn't think she could stop him.

That thought disturbed her deeply.

What were they supposed to do? She looked out the window.

The sloop had turned upstream into the mouth of the Saar River. Houses made way for farms and barns. The glow of fire lit up the fields and the willows. A herd of black-and-white cows stood at the riverbank with the glow of fire turning them pale orange. Their distraught moos echoed over the landscape.

The entire inner city was on fire. The palace was destroyed. Father's office, destroyed. Their house, destroyed.

Anger burned in her.

"We will get whoever did this. We will avenge whoever died here. We will avenge our king and queen."

"How do you know they're dead?" Nellie asked, her voice timid. "They might have fled like us."

"I saw the bodies," Johanna said. "They're all dead, most of the people who were in that hall."

"What about your father?"

Johanna shrugged. "I don't know." Her eyes clouded over.

"They're dead!" Roald cried. He sank to his knees, leaned his head against cabin wall, pushed himself off the wall and let himself fall back against the wood. His forehead hit the wall with a clunk.

Johanna gasped.

He did it again, and again.

"Your Highness, stop. Please stop!" She pulled at his shoulders, but he slipped from her grip and continued to bash his head.

Nellie looked as if she had seen a ghost. Her lips moved. *That is Prince Roald?*

He squealed, "All gone, all gone! Like my sister. Dead."

With every word, he bashed his forehead into the wall.

Johanna yelled, "Stop it!"

He'd hurt himself. She threw herself between the wall and his head. His forehead hit her hard in her right breast. She had to clamp her jaws to stop herself from yelping. He wailed and let himself slide to the floor. She fell, too, unbalanced by the movement, and collapsed on top of him. He was screaming and threshing about, hitting his hands on the legs of the chair.

Nellie started screaming, too.

"Be quiet, both of you!" Johanna screamed as loud as she could, while she struggled to pin Roald's arms down.

Nellie fell quiet and a moment later, Roald did the same. His eyes stared into nothingness. He was panting, his pale-skinned and hairless chest heaving rapidly. His lips moved but no sound came out. Chilling. Johanna had no idea what to do or what to say that would not set him off again. She knew nothing about people who weren't right in the head.

"Mistress Johanna?" Nellie said, timid.

Johanna glanced up at her, still keeping Roald down.

"Are you all right?"

"As soon as he calms down, I will be."

Nellie blinked, her eyes wide. "Mistress Johanna, do you know that you're wrestling the crown prince?"

"I guess I've noticed."

"But . . . but . . . you can't do that."

"I should have let him hurt himself?"

Nellie swallowed visibly. She was still staring at Roald as if he was something horrendously evil, like her brain was trying to process what Johanna already knew. "He isn't . . . he wouldn't . . ."

"I don't know what he would or wouldn't do. I don't know anything about his . . . condition."

Nellie backed further into the door. The words *I don't want to deal with an idiot* on her face. "But you can't . . ." Her chest moved in quick breaths. "He is . . ."

"All right, all right." Johanna released him, since he appeared to have calmed down.

Roald sat up straight and stared at Nellie, or rather, at her dress. A button had come undone. She looked down, noticed it. "Oh." She did it up, her cheeks going red, and then she curtsied. "Your Highness." But her face showed her fear.

"You have big tits."

"What?" Nellie's voice rose into a squeak.

"Tits. Boobs. That's what you call them, isn't it?"

"Your Highness—I . . ." She gasped and clamped her hands over her chest. Her eyes were so wide that the whites showed on all sides. Poor Nellie, she looked like she was going to faint. Johanna put her hand on her shoulder and guided her out of the cabin into the cramped galley. Between the furnace and the wall there was barely room for both of them.

Johanna whispered, "Calm down, Nellie. He's not aware of the effect of his words." Or maybe he *liked* the effect of his words. Her voice sounded muffled in the constricted space.

"But he's an . . ." She lowered her voice and whispered, ". . . idiot."

"He's the only member of the royal family left alive."

Nellie gulped. "But did you hear what he said. It's simply scandalous."

"Do you want to know what he said to me while we were dancing?"

Nellie brought her hands to her mouth. "So that is why Celine became crown princess."

Johanna nodded. "But he's all we have now. Nellie, please listen. I don't know what's happened in Saardam, who is still alive and who isn't, except I know the king and queen aren't. I don't know who the bandits are except that they came in revenge because the king did something. I think he hired a necromancer to bring back Celine."

"He couldn't have done that! That would be the worst of evil magic. He supports the Church."

"Unfortunately, that's what he did. The king gave his fortune to the Church because he believed that Celine would be resurrected, or that they would cure Roald. But the Shepherd couldn't do that, of course. When he says during mass that the dead will live on, he means that their spirits live on in us. The king believed that Celine would come back to life."

"Why didn't he ask one of Roald's cousins to step in as crown prince? I'm sure Prince Jona from Burovia would have been more than happy to come here."

"Because all of that part of the royal family don't agree with the Church and have disowned the king. I think it was the King's plan to make the Reverend Romulus regent on behalf of Roald, but leave Roald on the throne. In any case, I don't know what will happen, but chances are we three—four, with Loesie—will have to get along with each other. Let's try to behave nicely."

Nellie swallowed, opened her mouth and swallowed again. Her expression said, *But she's bewitched* and *He's an idiot* and *He said a scandalous thing to me*. But, small-minded as Nellie might be, she wasn't stupid, so she said only, "Where can we go?"

"First, we need to find somewhere Roald can be safe. If you go down the ladder just outside the door, you'll get into the hold. It's big, but it's dry and empty. You'll find some blankets and oiled cloth down there. See if you can make a bed for us. I'll tell Loesie to tie up at fisherman's corner. Then we'll see what we can do in the morning. The fires may have calmed down enough for us to go back." She didn't really think so, nor did she believe that the bandits would just walk away from their prize after conquering it, but she didn't want to frighten Nellie more than necessary.

Nellie nodded, her face pale, and left.

Johanna went back into the cabin, where Roald lay on his back on the narrow bed. How had she not noticed the stench of male sweat before?

"Your Highness . . . You can get up."

He pushed himself into a sitting position, his face sweat-slicked and haggard. He passed a hand through his rumpled hair. "I'm so tired." And then a bit later, "Everyone always says bad things about me."

"Who does?"

"That girl doesn't like me."

Like that was a surprise. Poor Nellie.

She sighed. She didn't have the time or energy to argue or try to explain what he probably wouldn't understand. For some reason, Queen Cygna's words about her son came to her *Roald is a good man. He doesn't always understand, but he would never harm anyone.*

That might be true, but he was completely obsessed with the other sex and the different parts of their anatomy.

"You can sleep here," she told him. The captain's bunk wasn't much—very narrow—and the cabin was tiny and definitely not fit for a prince.

Johanna backed to the door. "Well, goodnight, Your Highness."

"No!" His eyes were wide.

"What's the matter? You can go to sleep. I have to help

Loesie and Nellie. We have to get to a safe spot to tie up for the night."

"No, don't go. I need help."

Oh, she wanted to get out, because there was no way she was going to help him take off his trousers.

She backed to the door, stepped out and shut it. The last she saw was Roald sitting on the bed in his wet trousers.

The night air was cool and fresh. Loesie stood at the stern with the reins. Scuffling noises in the hold suggested that Nellie had found something to make a bed. Johanna joined Loesie at the bow, but everything seemed under control here. The entire horizon behind the boat lit up with orange light.

She had best check on Nellie.

When Johanna walked past the cabin, she glanced inside.

Roald still sat on the bed, his hands jammed between his knees, staring at the door. The only things that moved were his blinking eyelids. His face was utterly blank. He had not started to remove his clothes. Maybe he was used to people doing this for him. Maybe, with his simple mind, he didn't know how to do it.

A feeling of shame came over her.

Here was a young man confused and scared, who had lived hidden away from the world for most of his life. People might have told him that he was shameful and not worth anything. He'd lost his parents and was all alone, and this was how they treated him?

He frightened her, but that was not how she would want to be treated.

She braced herself and opened the door to the cabin.

"Your Highness, do you want me to help you?"

His expression remained blank.

A smile or some sort of reaction would have made her feel more comfortable, but she guessed the absence of a reaction was as good as an approval.

She knelt at his feet and undid shoelaces. They were wet, and she had to pull hard to get the knot out and even harder to get the shoes off his feet. His socks had lost shape with their soddenness. His feet were pale and slender, with long toes and clean nails, but the pads of his soles bore a few spots of callus. She wondered what he'd done to earn those.

Then she asked him to stand up, which he did without comment. Then she had to figure out how to undo his belt. The trousers were quite loose and fell down by themselves. Underneath he wore silken shorts with the Carmine Crest embroidered. Johanna had already decided enough was enough and there was no way she was going to bother with those. That would be asking for trouble. She never even saw Father in any state except fully clothed. Roald's legs were as thin as the rest of him. The skin had little pimples and a coating of blond hair. He had a rash on his upper legs. Was she meant to do anything about it?

His skin puckered in goose bumps. He had a few sparse chest hairs, but nowhere near the carpet she'd seen on the men who unloaded the ships.

She draped the blanket over him. "Come, Your Highness, get in the bed. You'll be warm."

He climbed awkwardly onto the narrow bed. Johanna draped the blankets over him and retreated to the door. "Well, goodnight. Sleep well."

He said, "I'm hungry. Can you get the cook to bring us some food?"

"We don't have a cook."

"What about the other girl? The one with dark hair and no tits."

"That girl is Loesie and she's steering the boat." It was going to be a very long trip if he kept talking about women like that.

"I'm hungry."

"We'll eat tomorrow." Once they got the furnace in the galley going and they were in a safe enough spot to stop.

"I want to go home."

"Me, too, but we can't."

"I want to go home. Why don't you take me home? That's what servants are for. That's what my father says: if you don't know what to do, ask the servants. They will help you. Is that right?"

"Yes, that's right, but I'm not a servant."

"Aren't you? But I thought . . ." He frowned at her, and then a spark of emotion lit his eyes. "I know. I remember you. You are going to be my wife."

"Your Highness?" Last he'd said was that he didn't want to marry her.

"I . . . I was only joking."

"Joking, Your Highness?" Her heart was thudding in her throat.

"I said you were ugly, but you aren't ugly. You're much prettier than the other girls."

"Um—thank you, Your Highness."

"But that doesn't matter now, does it? The other girls are dead. Everyone is dead." He rubbed his hands into his face and started sobbing. She positioned herself so that she could grab him if he started banging his head into the wall again.

"They're all dead. All dead!"

"Please, Your Highness . . ."

He didn't react. Johanna stood motionless in the cabin. Had he been a normal person, she might have sat on the bed and tried to comfort him, but he wasn't and he scared her.

"Come . . . Your Highness. Please go to sleep now." She felt so incredibly awkward. Mortified. She didn't want to touch him anymore. Not while he thought that she was going to marry him.

He looked up at the timber ceiling. There was a portrait of Mother in the cabin.

"This sloop is moving." It wasn't a question. He would know river travel from his trip to the sanatorium.

"It is."

"Where . . . where are we going?"

"For now, to find a safe spot. Then, to get help. To save Saarland from the barbarians."

"Yes." He nodded. "That's good."

"Well then, I should check on the others." She grabbed the door handle.

"No, don't go."

"Your Highness?" She stopped, wondering if she would ever be allowed to escape to freedom.

He patted the edge of the bed. "Sit here. My mother does that."

How embarrassing. Queen Cygna sat with her son until he fell asleep?

"Tell me a story."

"I . . . I don't know any stories."

"But I have to have a story. I can't sleep without a story."

Johanna forced herself to come up with some silly story about a cat which jumped aboard a ship in the orient and travelled the world. Letting her mind wonder through Father's tales was strangely relaxing. She felt certain that he was alive, and that many other people were still alive, and that they'd rebuild the city from the ashes and that they'd drive out the bandits. After all, what nation that could send ships across the high seas would not be able to defend itself and rebuild?

While she spoke, he stared at the ceiling, and gradually, his eyelids fell shut and his breathing became heavy and regular.

When Johanna was certain that he was asleep, she rose and tiptoed to the door.

Outside, it was pitch dark, with the glow of the burning city reduced to a thin stripe on the horizon.

The cool fingers of the night reached through her clothes. The water rippled against the sides of the boat and occasionally there would be a snort or a splash from one of the cows.

Johanna could only just make out Nellie's silhouette, holding onto the railing watching the fires. Loesie was a ghostly white spot at the bow.

"Did you find what you needed in the hold?" Johanna asked.

"I tried my best, but it's very dusty down there, mistress. I found a straw sack and some blankets. We won't get wet, and we may not get cold, but that's all there is to be said."

"Thank you, Nellie."

Johanna joined her at the railing. Neither of them said anything for a while.

"Mistress Johanna?" Nellie's voice sounded timid.

"Yes."

"I didn't know the rumours were true."

"What rumours?"

"That the prince . . . is a halfwit." She let a silence lapse. "I know it's a horrible word, but what else do I say?"

"I guess it's true enough."

"So that is why Celine was crown princess even though she was younger."

"Highly likely." It didn't really matter anymore, since everyone was gone. Roald needed a wife. He needed children. Without the Carmine House, Saarland would be reabsorbed into Estland or annexed by Burovia, and that would not be good for anyone.

"Poor Queen Cygna."

Johanna didn't reply. A chill crept over her as she remembered the Queen's open eyes.

"What are we going to do, Mistress Johanna? You know that friend of yours scares me."

"I know, Nellie, but Loesie is a good person."

"She's touched by the Lord of Fire."

"Magic, Nellie. Magic."

"Oh, Mistress Johanna, don't say that!" She made a unity with her hand and glanced skyward.

Johanna shrugged, but Nellie couldn't see that in the dark. What would they do? Johanna and Nellie, a witch struck mute by magic and the only surviving member of the royal family, who, it occurred to her, would be the official king in exile.

"I think we need to get Roald to safety. We need to find advisors for him. We need to have an official ceremony to make him the king. Important people have to witness it."

And then? With the demons in possession of Saardam, there would be war. If Roald was too simple to want to reclaim the city, someone else would. Surely someone was still alive in the city? Father? And what would they do?

And then a chill. What about the Church? Would everyone who supported the Church be killed by these bandits?

In the pale moonlight, the river showed up as a bright ribbon of silver. They were coming up to the loop called Fisherman's Bend, where a couple of other sloops lay moored. Fortunately no one was on deck.

Johanna helped Loesie guide the cows to a free pylon. Lifting the heavy rope over the top of the pylon was hard, with her arms as cold and sore as they were, but Johanna and Loesie managed it without bumping into any of the other boats.

Loesie worked silently next to her, and Johanna almost forgot her friend's condition.

"Let's go to sleep," she said, when the sloop was tied up, and the cows untangled from the harness and left to graze. Her arms ached, her eyes felt gritty with tiredness.

Nellie sat on the sloping cover to the hold. She eyed Loesie warily when they passed.

Loesie gave a sniff that made Nellie flinch. Irritated that she didn't help, Johanna guessed.

"You can look after breakfast tomorrow," Johanna said to Nellie.

She expected protests about not knowing how to light the fire and where things were, but Nellie said nothing.

Johanna was first to descend in the ink-black hold where the glow from the storm light barely made any impact. She found the bed that Nellie had improvised: a rough sack filled with straw that was normally spread in the bottom of the hold to absorb any cheese juices and was still relatively clean. Nellie had spread blankets over it.

No one undressed. Nellie was too scared of Loesie to want to sleep next to her, so Johanna went in the middle. She pulled the blankets and then the oiled cloth over her. Nellie took off her shoes and went on one side, Loesie on the other.

Getting to sleep, though, was another thing altogether.

The blanket was itchy and straw kept poking through the material of the sack. The *Lady Sara*, being empty, rode high in the water, and was tugged by the current of the river. The hull softly bumped against the pylons.

Several times, Johanna got up, climbed up the stairs to check if the sloop was still tied up, which it was, or if other people had come, which they hadn't.

And she didn't know whether to be happy or sad about it.

CHAPTER 15

JOHANNA AWOKE to a ray of light on her face, feeling cold and sore all over. She stared at the bottom of the doors of the empty hold, where normally grain was stored.

She sat up, pushing the oiled cloth aside, letting biting cold air touch her skin. A thin shard of light came into the hold from where the cover had been left ajar. There was no sound except the slapping of water.

Nellie was still asleep next to her, wearing her clothes and resting her head on a pile of empty grain sacks. Loesie was gone.

Johanna rose. Her clothes were damp from the cloying humidity. She draped the cloth—normally used to cover the cargo in the hold—back over Nellie, who stirred. Her face, pale and smudged, scrunched briefly, but relaxed again as she rolled onto her back.

Poor Nellie.

Johanna clambered up the rickety ladder to the deck. The countryside around the boat was delicate green under a thick layer of mist. The mooring ropes were tied to a couple of mooring posts that were normally used by barges to wait until they could come into harbour. Last night there had been two other boats, but they had gone.

There was a small beach and reeds to the sides. A couple of ducks paddled along the edge of the reed bed.

The most eerie thing was the complete silence. The church bells had stopped ringing. If anyone was still shouting, their voices were inaudible from here. That raised the question: was there anyone left to shout at all?

Over the misty paddocks, she could see palls of smoke still rising from the city, although the flames would not be visible in daylight. From a distance the devastation looked oddly peaceful.

She could see no signs of life.

Loesie sat hunched at the captain's bench, with an oiled cloth over her shoulders, staring motionless over the river-bank. When Johanna came up to her, she started to sag side-ways, then gasped and pulled herself upright. She looked around in a confused way.

Johanna sat down next to her. She had done a good job in detaching the sea cow harness from the stern and loosening their individual harnesses. The cows were grazing on the bottom, stirring up clouds of murky water punctuated with bubbles. Wherever there were sea cows, there were always bubbles.

"Have you seen anyone?"

Loesie shook her head.

"Any other ships?"

She shook her head again. Her face was pale and smudged.

"You go and have a sleep. I'll take over."

She rose and only then Johanna noticed a rusted knife in her hands.

"What are you doing with that thing? You said there was no one here."

Loesie clutched the weapon to her chest. "Ghghghghghghgh!" There was a wild look in her eyes.

"Whoa, calm down. I'm not going to do anything to you." Johanna held her hands up, heart thudding. For a moment, it was as if Loesie hadn't recognised her.

"Ghghghghghgh!" Loesie's voice sounded distressed. There were tears in her eyes.

She backed away slowly until she was a few paces away from Johanna, then turned on her heel and ran.

Nellie was just climbing out of the hold, and Loesie almost crashed into her. Nellie gave a startled shout when Loesie pushed past and disappeared into the hold.

Nellie strode to Johanna's side, her cheeks red. "That's what I mean, Mistress Johanna. She doesn't act like a normal person."

"There's nothing I can do about it," Johanna said. She both agreed with Nellie that there was something disturbingly wrong with Loesie, and wished she'd stop complaining. "Loesie is my friend. I'm not going to abandon her."

Nellie gave her the *I-never-approved-of-this-friend* look.

Good grief! If it wasn't for Loesie, they might all be dead along with a lot of other people in town.

Johanna let herself drop on the wooden shutters that covered the hold. The willow wood sang to her. It showed her smoke drifting through an orange sky. The glow from the fires reflected in the slow-flowing water of the river. There had been a shower overnight and now the banks of the river were cloaked in mist. The road along the river glistened with puddles.

The planks moved when Nellie sat down next to her.

"I'm sorry. I don't really want to abandon anyone either. I

shouldn't have said that." She folded her hands in her lap. "But she does scare me. What is wrong with her?"

Johanna sighed. "I wish I knew."

Whatever had been done to Loesie scared her, too. Whoever had done it, and why. The images from the wood had shown her bears, and the body of a woman. She now wished that she had the basket Loesie had given her, since the magic faded from them after a few weeks, and, knowing what she knew now, she would like to see the images again.

"Have you seen anyone this morning?" Nellie asked. She scanned the horizon where mist cloaked the burning city. "Is anyone still alive?" Her voice sounded small.

"I don't know."

But at that moment, there was a faint sound of a whistle behind them. Johanna turned into the light of the early sun. Something moved on the road that led into town. She went into the galley to get the spyglass.

"What is it, Mistress Johanna? Can you see something?"

Johanna put the spyglass to her eye. The eyepiece fogged up but she wiped it with her dress.

"There." She pointed at the riverbank, where the group of men was coming over a ridge, towards the city. There were at least fifty of them. Many of them rode horses. She could see no bears.

"I see them too. Can you see who they are?"

Johanna studied the people, still too far away to recognise faces. The view field of the spyglass was not very big and it was hard to hold it still for long enough to study individual people. They were also silhouetted against the sun. But several people wore furs or dark clothing. They also had dogs, hence the whistling.

"I don't know. It doesn't look good. Let's hide in the cabin. I don't want to be seen when they get here." Especially not with Prince Roald aboard.

They went into the galley, which had a small window to the side. Pressed against each other so that they could both see, Johanna and Nellie watched the group ride past: rugged men in leather jerkins with long and untidy hair, laughing and talking as if they owned the world. They were bandits.

Johanna only dared speak once they had passed. "They've occupied the town."

"Where are they from?"

"My guess: Burovia." But gangs of Burovian forest bandits would never come this far out of their usual home. Someone had to have ordered them here. Someone who was holding these bands of rogues together in a way they had never been before. And for some reason—was it just something that King Nicholaos had done?—they decided to invade.

"Do you still think we can go back home?"

Johanna shook her head. "Not now. Not with the prince. If they killed his parents, they'd have no trouble killing him. We need to make sure he's safe first."

Nellies eyes grew wide. "Then what are we going to do?"

"We should go the Aroden castle. The duke will help us. The castle will be a safe place for the prince while we find out what is going on in the city." Not to mention that her uncle lived there. He would surely help her find Father. "Come on, let's get going."

She rose and went to the bow where Loesie had tied up the harness and the individual ropes that held each of the cows. A standard team consisted of eight animals. The pull beam that stuck out the front of the boat had a central bar and eight cross-bars, each with a set of slots for the ropes that went from the cow's harness to the bow.

She untied the ropes and slowly reeled the animals in, one at a time. She asked Nellie to guide the ropes into the slots, and tie them off at the bar on the deck, but her knots were awkward and it was clear she had never done anything like this.

Neither, for that matter, had Johanna. She spent a long time getting cows into their right positions in the team. All she knew was that you started from the front, but the animals must have known that she was inexperienced, because they twisted the ropes and went into the wrong places, tangling up their harnesses. There was, she remembered too late, some sort of hierarchy in the team. The dominant animals were supposed to be at the front, but how could she workout which ones they were? One sea cow looked pretty much like the other.

Nellie stood helplessly to the side. The one time that she tried to help, she almost fell off the boat. Since Johanna didn't think Nellie could swim, she told Nellie to keep out of the way.

Meanwhile, the sun rose and rose. A couple of horses and carts came past, but most of those Johanna judged to be local farm traffic. They had to get moving.

"Look, can you go and get Loesie to help us?" she asked Nellie.

Nellie left and Johanna continued struggling with the tangling ropes and the cheeky cows.

There was a scream.

Johanna jerked around, letting the rope slip from her fingers.

"Nellie!"

She came running towards Johanna. Her cheeks were red. "Oh, Mistress Johanna, it's awful. The prince . . ."

Roald. Her heart thumped. Something had happened to Roald. They'd forgotten to give him pills or some other medicine. "Is he all right?"

She made for the cabin, but Nellie held her back. "Yes, he's fine but you can't see him like this."

"What is wrong, Nellie?"

She burst into tears. "The prince . . . the prince . . ."

What?

"Calm down, Nellie. Tell me. Sit down." Johanna sat her on the edge of the cover of the cargo hold. She was shaking and shivering. Tears were running over her cheeks.

"The prince," Johanna prompted. She glanced at the horizon. They should really get out of here soon.

"I went to get the witch, as you said—"

"Loesie. Use her name."

"Loesie. I walked past the cabin, and the door opened. The prince came out, and he . . ." Her eyes widened. "He was in his underclothes. Scandalous!"

Johanna breathed out a heavy sigh and had to restrain herself from rolling her eyes. *He was in his underclothes!* Good grief. "Come on, Nellie. There's no time to worry about indecency. We need to hurry."

"But Mistress Johanna, I can't. I don't know how to say this: he tried to touch me. Indecently." She hid her face in her hands. "He grabbed me from behind, and he . . ." Her voice dissolved into sobs.

Oh, no. "Did he . . . hurt you?"

"No. I . . . hit him and I pushed him away. Oh, Johanna, I hit the crown prince."

"Did he seem upset when you hit him?"

"No. He laughed at me. But I hit the crown prince!"

"Calm down, Nellie. Sit here. I'll talk to him. But first, we have to get going. Here, hold onto these ropes, then I will get Loesie."

Johanna wobbled along the narrow walkway, her legs uncertain. It was one thing talking to Nellie like she knew what to do, but another having to deal with the problem. Roald was a man and he was strong even though he didn't look it. What would she do when he tried to grab her?

The door to the cabin was closed again. Fortunately. She'd deal with this later. There was no time now.

Johanna found Loesie under the oiled cloth in the hold. She lay down, but turned her head when Johanna came down the ladder. Her grey eyes blinked at the light.

"I'm sorry to keep you from your sleep, but I need your help. We need to get going, but I can't handle the sea cows by myself."

Loesie pushed herself up, attempting to straighten her dishevelled clothes. Johanna didn't like the look in her eyes. Far-off, not really there. Not herself at all. What was going on in that mind of hers?

"I want to go to Aroden castle. We'll be safe there. But I can't get the cows in the harnesses by myself." She almost said something about Nellie being useless, but that felt unkind. Nellie had never any experience in things like this, and Johanna couldn't blame her. But she was a nuisance. Once they got going, Nellie would be able to make herself useful by cooking, but even that meant Johanna had to get the furnace going, because Nellie wouldn't know how to do that.

There was so much to do. Normally, the *Lady Sara* had a captain and a minimum of four competent deck hands who knew what they were doing.

Loesie threw off the covers and accompanied Johanna up the ladder, past the door to the cabin—still closed—and to the front of the boat. She hissed and hmmmed and pointed at the rope harnesses. Yes, Johanna had probably gotten it all wrong.

Under Loesie's direction, they managed to get each animal tied up to their individual bars in the beam. Loesie untied the mooring ropes and hauled them in. Feeling the pressure against their backs, the cows started swimming. Johanna flung the bait into the water to keep them going and the boat slowly started moving. Johanna scanned the river-banks, but could no longer see any people.

Next, the furnace.

She went into the galley. Next to the furnace lay a stack of peat bricks and a basket of kindling. She put kindling and one fire brick inside the stove, then stuck a stick from the kindling basket into the glowing coals of the firebox. When it burned, she used it to light the kindling. Soon, the fire was going.

Meanwhile, she'd gone through the cupboards in the galley and found a pan, a couple of battered plates and an assortment of cutlery. There was also a bag of oats, so they could make porridge. She was beginning to get very hungry. She left Nellie to this task, because it was high time to look after Roald.

She knocked on the door that connected the galley and the cabin. "Your Highness? Do you need any help?"

A muffled voice came through the wood. "If you're that crazy woman, then don't come in."

Nellie said, "That's what he's been saying all along, Mistress Johanna, and he's talking about me. He—"

Johanna shushed her and opened the door. Roald sat at the edge of his bed, wearing nothing but his underpants.

Nellie shrieked.

Roald laughed.

"Calm down, calm down, Nellie." But she noticed the skin on his chest, mostly hairless, but with a distinct tan. His arms were thin but with corded muscles. This probably accounted for the strength he had shown climbing up the side of the sloop last night. There was no way any of the women could win a physical argument with him, if he decided to do some-thing stupid and if they needed to stop him.

His eyes, startlingly blue, met hers. He gave a dumb grin.

Johanna's cheeks grew warm. Had he no shame? "Are you all right, Your Highness?"

"I'm hungry. Where is breakfast?"

"We're working on it."

"I want breakfast. They always bring me breakfast at this time. Where are the servants in this place?"

"There are none. We're on a boat on the river. We should be lucky that we're still alive, but you're going to have to be a little bit more patient for breakfast."

"I'm hungry." His voice was angrier.

"Yes. We're hungry, too. Breakfast is coming." *It just might not be what you expect.* "But first, you must get dressed. You can't have breakfast like this. Wait, I'll get your clothes."

She went back into the galley, where Nellie was scrubbing the inside of the pan with a piece of cloth. Her cheeks were red with the effort.

"What are you doing?"

"This pan is disgusting."

"I'm sure that doesn't matter for once." It was only stained anyway.

"I'm not going to eat breakfast out of anything this dirty."

"The porridge will be cooked! Come on, Nellie, everyone is hungry! It doesn't matter."

"It matters to me. Everyone stop screaming at me! I can't do this. I'm useless." She let go of the pan, which fell to the floor with a clang. She hid her face in her hands and started sobbing.

Great. She was stuck on this boat with a prince who wanted to be served, a witch who couldn't speak and a maid who had fallen to pieces.

Johanna picked up the pan, filled it with water and set it on the stove. Then she turned to Nellie.

"Listen to me, Nellie. You're going to do this. This is not what

I would have chosen to do today either, but this is what we've got. I, for one, would love to know where Father is." She had to pause because her voice threatened to crack. "But we've got other responsibilities. You and I are the only sane people on this ship and we're going to have to keep it together. So you're going to do your share of work, and stop complaining about things we can't do anything about, and just stop being prissy or I'll push you overboard. And I mean it!" Her voice had become louder while she was speaking, and the last sentence rang in the silence.

Nellie started at her. She opened her mouth, licked her lips and closed it again. "You wouldn't really do that, Mistress Johanna?"

Johanna shrugged. She felt ashamed. It was the first time ever she'd screamed at Nellie. She was losing it as well.

"Look, we're all tired and hungry. Make the porridge. We'll stop at a farm to see if we can barter something in return for some eggs or milk. I need Roald's clothes. Where did you hang them?"

"They were in front of the stove but I had to move them. They're not dry."

She handed Johanna a heavy bundle. The heavy velvet jacket was as wet as it had been last night. The shirt had some dry patches, but it was badly stained. The trousers were also still soaked.

"He can't wear this. He'll get sick."

"We don't have anything else."

"Can you hang it closer to the fire so it can dry?"

Nellie looked like she wanted to protest again, but she thought the better of it and took the coat and trousers from Johanna.

She took the shirt into the cabin. They really needed to get different clothes because, for his safety, Roald couldn't be seen in the Carmine jacket, but she didn't know that any of them had money, and the nearest river towns were not until they reached Estland. If they got that far.

"I'm sorry, Your Highness, the rest of your clothes are still very wet."

He took the shirt from her without a word. Made no attempt to put it on. His naked skin was covered in goose bumps, but it didn't seem to bother him.

"If you want breakfast, you're going to have to put the shirt on."

He simply spread his arms.

So, she had to do that for him as well, huh? She shook out the shirt in order to hide that it wasn't completely dry. In fact, damp was probably a better word for it. Yet he didn't flinch or shiver when she put his arms in and pulled the shirt over his shoulders.

While she did up the buttons, he glanced at the door. "Where is the crazy woman?"

"You mean Nellie?" Seriously, he was getting under her skin. Didn't anyone teach him manners? "She's not crazy. She's very upset that you touched her. You shouldn't do that anymore."

A small frown crossed his face. "I can't touch a girl? My father said that the whole country would be mine, with all the girls in it."

Well, your father was wrong, then. Good grief. "It is not appropriate to go around touching women, even if they are the women of your country. The women may be married to someone else, and the other person won't be happy."

"Oh." His frown deepened. "My father says I should get married. Are you married?"

"No, I am not, but—" Had he already forgotten that his father was dead? Did he understand what *dead* meant?

"If I marry you I can touch you, right?"

"Yes, but—"

"Then we should get married. I want to touch a woman."

"Maybe you should discuss that with your court advisors. A crown prince doesn't just marry the first girl he comes across."

"Oh, you mean the Reverend Romulus?"

Since when was he a court advisor? "Yes, if you want."

"Is he married?"

"No. He's a priest."

"Then how can he tell me what I should do?"

Johanna couldn't restrain a snort of laughter. "You best never let him hear that."

He giggled. "You think it's funny I said that?"

"It's not appropriate."

"When something is funny, it's never appropriate."

Johanna laughed aloud; she couldn't help it.

He gave a squeal. "You think I'm funny!" He slapped his thigh. "A woman thinks I'm funny. The other ones just sneak into my room and bow." He put on a high voice. "Your majesty, do you want tea? Do you want me to do up your shoelaces? Ha ha ha ha!"

He did such a convincing imitation of a courtier that Johanna laughed again.

"Shh, Your Highness, sit still so I can do up the buttons."

Laughing felt good. How nice it would be to be able to forget the horrific scenes from last night and the hopeless situation they found themselves in. Roald didn't really care. He was incapable of caring or had a short memory. Who knew what went on in his head? Because clearly, something went on in there and while he was certainly odd and childish, *stupid* was not how she'd describe him.

She did up the buttons on his shirt.

"I'm sorry, but your trousers are still really wet. I've asked Nellie to hang them close to the furnace."

He rose. "That doesn't matter. I don't like wearing them anyway."

"But you can't go outside like this. And you'll be cold." She looked around the cabin and her gaze rested on an empty grain sack that was tucked under the desk. "I can make you a skirt out of this, so at least you can go into the fresh air." Some of the Burovian warriors wore short skirts.

She crawled under the desk to retrieve the sack, aware of his keen gaze on her backside.

Did people in the palace really dress him every day? Did his mother do that for him? Surely he didn't treat all female courtiers like this. Did he? And they put up with that behaviour?

His waist was very slender and the sack fitted around him like a skirt. With great embarrassment, she noticed how his underwear strained in his crotch. Heavens.

She took his belt and looped it around his waist. "There." She stepped back looking at her handiwork.

"See? I didn't touch you."

Thank heavens.

"But I want to touch you."

"No, you can't."

"Why not?"

"Because I'm not a cheap woman."

"I have money. Lots of it. That's what sailors do, right?"

She cringed. "No, Your Highness, because you are not a sailor. You are a prince."

He let himself fall back on the bed in a theatrical gesture. "Being a prince is boring." He sighed. "If I'm nice, will you let me touch you?"

"Your Highness, you shouldn't speak of touching women all the time. That's not—" She'd almost said *appropriate* again, but she realised he probably had no idea of what it meant. That was his problem. He did not understand *appropriate*.

"Touching women is very special. You don't talk about it with other people."

"Oh, like a secret?"

"Yes." Fine, if that got him to shut up.

"Oh, I like secrets. Can it be our secret? You and me?"

"Um—I suppose." She was desperate to get out of here.

At that moment, there was a squeal from the galley.

What now?

Johanna opened the door. Nellie stood at the stove staring at smoke rising from the pan. "Oh look, Mistress Johanna. This is much too hot!"

Johanna bent over the pan. Blackened porridge coated the bottom of it. This was probably why the pan had been dirty in the first place: it was too thin for cooking on hot fires.

Nellie cried, "What can I do now? What are we going to eat? I have to start all over again!" She wiped her cheeks.

"Calm down, Nellie."

"But you all think I'm stupid. I don't know what I'm doing today. I'm not a cook, but—"

Roald came into the galley. He picked up the smoking pan and poked at the bottom with a spatula that hung above the stove. He scraped some of the blackened porridge away.

Johanna retreated, pushing Nellie out the side door onto the deck, still sniffing.

Roald scraped all the burnt bits into a heap and tossed them on the sideboard of the stove. Then he took a chipped cup from the back shelf and filled it with water. He tipped this into the pan. He measured out oats from the sack and tipped this into the water.

"You can't put too much oats in," he said, and his voice sounded definitive.

Nellie turned to Johanna, frowning. "He knows how to cook?"

Johanna put her finger to her lips.

That the prince wasn't entirely normal also didn't mean that he couldn't listen. In fact, she suspected that he could do just that very well.

Somewhere in that Burovian sanatorium, he had clearly learned to cook camp meals. Johanna suspected that sanatorium was probably not the right word for where he had been. He seemed to have spent a lot of time outdoors.

Not much later, all four of them sat on the covers of the hold, eating bland and watery but steaming hot porridge. Until then, Johanna had not realised how hungry she was and how much it affected her mood. They ate until there was nothing left in the pan. When she finished, Johanna lay back on the sloping surface of the cover, watching the clouds track through the sky.

Nellie sat with her knees pulled up against her chest, looking miserable. Loesie had stayed a bit away from the group, while Roald was using his fingers to scrape every last bit of porridge from the plate.

"It was good. Thank you," she said, but he continued licking the bowl and didn't react.

"It wasn't good. It needs honey." He still didn't look at anyone.

"We don't have honey."

"I want honey. Tell the kitchen staff to order honey."

CHAPTER 16

THE SLOOP MOVED upriver at a steady pace. The mist rose mid-morning and the sun came out.

It was spring, the time when the river swelled and spread into the surrounding paddocks. The sea cows found it hard going and their movement was slow. Fortunately, also because of the water, no one on the riverbanks could get close enough to the *Lady Sara* to see who was on board.

A few boats met them coming down the river. Some of them Johanna even recognised, but they couldn't stop and after a few attempts, she had to give up trying to warn them of the events in Saardam, judging that it was probably better not to draw attention to themselves for Roald's safety. Women didn't crew river sloops, and they would be very visible even if only because of that.

Between themselves, they gathered up anything that they could barter with farmers along the river in return for food, more comfortable clothes, sheets, blankets and, at Roald's insistence, honey.

It was depressing to see how little they had.

They could not possibly give away Roald's Carmine jacket, although it was more brown than red after its encounter with the brackish harbour water. He did have his pretty ruffled shirt and belt with an elaborate buckle. Johanna had no idea if it had any significance. But the jacket definitely did, and if anything, he needed something less conspicuous.

Johanna had a necklace and a brooch that was her mother's, but she would rather work hard labour than trade either one.

Nellie had a few coins from their visit to the markets. She also had a small prayer book. "But please, Mistress Johanna, only show it when we couldn't possibly survive without selling it." She had tears in her eyes.

"We may need it badly," Johanna said, although she had no idea how much of a market they would find in Estland for a book of Triune prayers.

Even if Estland hadn't been hostile to the Church, people in the country usually lived by the rising and setting of the sun, and the seasons, and the cycles of growth and death, helped by magic or not. They didn't need the Church. And more likely than not, they couldn't read. A book of prayers wouldn't be worth much to those people.

Roald had his seal ring and a heavy gold chain, but nothing of value that wouldn't immediately give away his identity, or raise the suspicion of people likely to think that they had stolen those things.

Tendrils of mist still drifted over the river, restricting their view to the willows on both banks, the reedy riverbanks, and brown churning water disappearing out of view. There were no other people, no houses. Small islands went by, green with buttercups, grazing cows and the occasional rabbit.

There were no villages along the river, but in the afternoon, they found a mooring post in a river bend. There was a little beach surrounded by waving reeds and a path that led up the riverbank. The truncated stems of a couple of willows showed that people lived nearby who cut the trees regularly to make baskets. The mooring post, too, meant that there was a farmhouse or small settlement, probably just on the other side, from which farmers loaded cheeses onto the passing sloops.

"Let's stay here for the night," she said. They wouldn't get to Aroden castle or even Estland today. Johanna wasn't even sure how to tell that they were in Estland, or how far it was. She wished she'd paid more attention when she came this way with Father.

Loesie steered the sea cow team into the still water. She handed Johanna the rope and Johanna managed to catch the post with the loop on the end, but when the line snapped taut, it almost pushed her into the water. She just managed to hang onto the rope. That was silly, standing where she did, in the way of the rope.

Loesie laughed, an eerie panting sound that made a chill run down Johanna's back. She stared at her friend. It was almost as if Loesie had done that on purpose.

Johanna ran a second rope to the jetty so the sloop wouldn't swing too much. They loosened the ropes on the sea cows' harnesses so they could graze. Most of them swam off towards the reeds.

All this was done without exchanging a single word. Loesie couldn't speak, of course, but Nellie also said nothing, seated on top of the shutters that covered the hold. She met Johanna's eyes, looking utterly miserable. Roald was in the cabin, probably asleep.

Then Loesie said, "Ghghghghgh!" She pointed at the riverbank.

Johanna peered. "What's the matter?" She couldn't see anything on the bank except grass. No, there was a young willow tree in amongst the reeds.

"Do you want me to look at the wood?"

Loesie nodded, and her expression was anxious. The chill that Johanna had felt earlier came back. Maybe it wasn't to do with Loesie. Maybe something bad had happened here.

Johanna stepped from the deck onto the jetty. She knelt and placed her palm flat on the planks, but if they had ever told a story, it had dissipated long ago.

She walked towards the shore, where the jetty went through the reeds into the grassy bank. Her footsteps sounded loud on the wood.

A path led from the jetty up the river bank and the flattened grass on both sides showed that someone had come this way perhaps as recently as this morning, but no longer ago than yesterday.

Johanna turned off the path. Wading through the knee-length grass, the bottom of her dress became wet. The willow tree stood in a soggy patch of land. Johanna disturbed a coot, which flew up with a loud shriek that made her heart beat like crazy.

Phew. Stupid to get so excited over a simple bird. She was so tense.

The trunk of the tree, a mere sapling, was wet from the mist. Johanna closed her eyes, but all it showed her was greyness. Did that mean no one had come here recently, or that there had been too much mist to see it?

Then she waded back through the grass to the jetty. She wanted to follow the path to see if they could find some people, but she couldn't go alone.

Who would she take?

Loesie could handle the boat, and could stay here, but Johanna didn't trust her. She might take off with the boat and then they would be lost. Nellie wouldn't do anything stupid, but Roald might do something stupid to her. Loesie didn't care that he was the crown prince and he was oblivious to her, so she and Roald seemed better matched in an odd sort of way. That made Nellie the best to stay on board, not that it sat well with her, either. Nellie could do nothing if someone came.

She heaved the bag with the few things they had to trade onto her shoulder.

"But what if there are bandits?" Nellie looked uncertain, standing at the deck.

"Just don't show yourself," Johanna said. "We'll be back as soon as we can."

While Johanna led Loesie and Roald up the path, Nellie walked to the back deck, and climbed down the ladder into the hold.

The sun came out, and instantly, the grass turned brighter green. Johanna noticed dandelions and daisies she hadn't noticed before. A lark did its singing dance high into the sky.

But then Johanna cleared the top of the riverbank.

A blackened, burnt-out shell stood where there had once been a farmhouse. The roof had fallen in and blackened beams pointed at the sky like ribs in a rotting corpse. A smell of fire gone out days ago drifted over the meadow, full of green grass and buttercups. There was a barn, also burnt out, in the middle of a vegetable garden with neat rows of seedlings. Daisies, poppies and cornflowers bloomed in the edges around the garden like a parody on the scene of death.

Loesie made a soft hissing sound, and Roald stared, his expression so empty that it chilled her.

"By the heavens . . ." Johanna raised her hand over her mouth.

A rutted track led past the farmhouse past marshy ground. On the other side stood the burnt-out remains of a mill, with a few more burnt-out houses. A wisp of smoke still trailed from one of them.

A few cows lay peacefully under a tree and a couple of

sheep grazed in a paddock, but she could see no other sign of people.

"Come," she said to Roald and Loesie. "We need to help survivors."

A little voice inside her said, *What if there are no survivors?*

An entire village murdered.

What would they find further upstream? Where did the destruction end?

They walked down the field. At the back of what was left of the farmhouse, sheets and clothes were flapping on the clothesline.

"See if there is anything that fits us," Johanna said. "Get all of it, including the sheets."

Loesie went into the garden and Johanna continued past the burnt-out shell of the house, with Roald following her like a little duckling.

She looked in through the opening where the door had been, which now lay in burnt pieces on the ground. The room was a kitchen, with the remains of a table and chairs in the middle. Shelves and a simple cupboard had been reduced to a pile of burnt planks.

Amongst the blackened ruins were some items that had strangely remained untouched. A bowl, half of a broom.

The air smelled strongly of stale wood smoke.

There was a charred lump on the floor, with bits of fabric adhering. Next to it was a smaller lump, with bits of a pink blanket.

Bile rose in her mouth when she realised what she was seeing. A mother and a child, burnt to coal.

With a trembling hand, she reached for a beam of wood. It must have been a roof beam, because she could see the surrounding of the house.

The attackers had come in the morning along the road that led past the mill, a group of men in leather jerkins and furs riding horseback, in the company of three bears. They carried flaming torches. At the mill, they stopped. One went in and threw the flaming torch in to the barn. A man ran out, and was attacked by a bear. His screams rang in her ears.

Johanna jerked her hand back from the wood, breaking the vision. The wood was crying for these people, mindlessly slaughtered by barbarians. They were innocent peasants. Whatever the king had done, nothing justified this mindless slaughter.

She leaned against the wall, her head reeling.

"Do you think they have honey?" Roald stepped over the remains of the door and went into the kitchen. He paid no heed to the bodies on the floor.

On the other side of the kitchen was another door that led into the pantry. Roald went in, ducking his head under a ceiling beam that had fallen cross the door.

There were clanging noises inside, and a moment later he came out carrying a pan filled with a few jars.

He showed the contents to her. "Look, there are peas. I like peas. And apples."

The contents of the pan consisted of a mix of foodstuffs in jars, most of them looking slightly smoked from the fire. There were dried apples, some potatoes, dried beans, flour and eggs.

"And look, there is honey."

There was, too. Roald's cheerful expression was eerily at odds with the horrible situation.

"Please, Your Highness. People have died here. Did you see the bodies on the floor?"

He frowned and looked over his shoulder. And said nothing for a while. Johanna didn't want to look at the mother and child again. She still felt queasy from the memory.

"Oh," he said eventually, although he didn't sound convinced.

"That's all? People died for you, or for what your father did. It was none of their fault. Can you show some respect?"

He turned to her. He had a smear of soot on his face. "But . . ." He frowned. "You said to get food. Aren't you happy?"

Hadn't he heard what she said? She breathed in to say something angry, but let her breath out again. It would be a waste of time. His mind seemed unable to deal with the feelings of others. Either he didn't understand them, or didn't notice them, or he had to act like this to cope with what had happened to him. Who knew how he had been treated for most of his life?

"Yes, I'm happy that you got food."

He flashed a childish, innocent smile that made her choke up. Imagine the bliss of not being able to comprehend the horror of this invasion.

Loesie had taken all the washing off the line. There were sheets, trousers and shirts.

Next to the burnt-out barn they found a wheelbarrow that was still useable. They piled the sheets and clothes in, together with the pan and its contents, and went to the other houses.

In the forecourt of the village lord's house, they disturbed a group of crows picking at a corpse. Neither of them felt inclined to look closer. The sweet scent of decay told the story louder than anything else could.

The house next to the mill was unaffected by fire, yet still uninhabited. Inside they found sacks of grain and some flour, but also some cheeses and a smoked ham, as well as plates, cups and tableware.

They found a metal bucket and went to milk the cows.

There were also a blankets and sheets neatly folded on shelves in the wardrobe.

The miller had to be a newly-married man, for everything in the house was fresh and there was not enough of it for an entire family.

Johanna felt terrible going through another person's house and stealing their possessions, but the little voice in her head said that the people themselves were unlikely to be able to use it.

But what if anyone has survived?

This happened days ago, they would already have come back if they were alive.

It was true, and the thought that all these people had just been killed was too big to comprehend.

Why would anyone do that?

They piled everything into the wheelbarrow and pushed it back through the waving grass. The sun was at its highest and when they came over the rise, the *Lady Sara* looked peaceful, as if they were simply underway to Lurezia and nothing had happened.

Nellie sat on deck, peering anxiously at the riverbank.

"We have food and clothes," Johanna shouted up to her.

They clambered up the ladder. They fashioned one of the horse blankets into a sack so they could haul the supplies up. The sack was heavy, but Roald took the rope from her and seemed to have little trouble with its weight. He lifted the sack to the deck. When he unwrapped the blanket, his eyes glittered like a child's.

"Look, we have cheese, I like cheese." He held the cheese out to Nellie, who almost dropped it. "You like ham? We have ham, too. And eggs. You have to be careful with them, or they'll break."

Loesie stood a little back, as if she was hesitant. Throughout the expedition she hadn't once tried to communicate. The look in her eyes chilled Johanna. Empty, vacant, as if her mind was being consumed from within.

"Did you see anyone while we were away?" Johanna asked Nellie.

She shook her head.

Johanna told Nellie about the burnt-out farmhouse.

"And what happened to the people who live here?"

"They're all dead. And if they're not, they're somewhere else. It was horrible, Nellie." Her voice wavered. She was tired, she wanted to know where Father was, and wanted to see at least one town that was unscathed.

They cut the cheese with one of the knives they had brought from the farmhouse, and ate from the plates that they'd found in the miller's house. Nellie put a sheet on the bed in the cabin and kept one for the two of them. They climbed down and got some hay to fashion into a bed in the hold.

When it grew dark, they snuggled under the new blankets.

"They're much warmer," Nellie said.

Johanna lay down, staring at the small gap of moonlight that peeped in between the covers.

She could still see the burnt corpses. A woman with a baby on the floor, white skulls in black ash, a piece of pink blanket. "What sort of monsters would do a thing like this? What sort of monsters would burn an entire city? Why?"

"I don't know, Mistress Johanna, but I'm scared." She breathed out heavily. "Your friend scares me. I think the prince is also possessed by evil."

"The prince is ill. He has always been like this." As for Loesie, yes Johanna could agree with her.

"You know how the Church says . . . the Shepherd says there isn't any magic? You have never believed that, haven't you?"

"You cannot deny what you know to exist. The Church may not like it, but magic exists."

She wondered what had brought this change in Nellie. "People who work on the land know it. Many have the magic. Many see the magic. It helps them grow their crops and look after their animals. If the Shepherds left their churches and got their noses out of their holy books, they would see that magic is all around."

"I never saw it."

"Then you also never looked, or didn't want to see it. This terrible disaster started with magic, it's wrought by magic and it's about magic. Turning away from magic does no one any good."

CHAPTER 17

THEY SAW NO ONE on the river the next day. No merchant sloops, no farmers' barges. Once they came past a punt moored on a jetty, but there were no people. When Johanna had come with Father to Lurezia, the river had been quite busy with merchants and other vessels. On that trip, there had been people crossing the river in small boats, people riding horses on the banks, people fishing. This time, it was as if the country had died.

Towards the end of the day, they arrived at the fork where the Rede River joined the Saar River. Both rivers were wide, softly churning expanses of water, and the Rede River especially was brown with the extra water from molten snow. The country on the left-hand bank would now be Estland, that on the right still Saarland. Past the Rede River, the left-hand bank would be Burovia. The tongue of land at the point between the two rivers was a kind of no-man's land that was claimed by Estland, Saarland, Burovia or even Gelre depending on who was speaking. It was marshy ground, not worth much except for its strategic position.

Upriver from the fork, the Saar River curved around in a

big loop. Loesie's farm was there, in an area people called The Bend.

Johanna stood at the bow looking over the vast expanse of water while the sea cows made slow progress through the churning water.

Aroden castle was on the Rede River, so they kept to the left.

Past the fork where the Rede River joined, the country became more hilly and the river faster. Dark swathes of forest spread on both banks.

Johanna had never been here. This had been considered dangerous country until quite recently. She had not attended the Aroden court for that reason, but had heard enough from Father about the bandits who would raid ships and steal all the cargo.

The *Lady Sara* continued up the river. Progress was slow because the current was strong and they had to make regular stops to rest the cows. Loesie mostly kept to looking after the cows and the ship. Nellie cleaned and tidied, even things that didn't need cleaning and tidying. Roald was happy to do most of the cooking, and turned to be decent at it, albeit very messy, which then annoyed Nellie because she had to clean up after him.

This left Johanna with precisely nothing to do except worry about the lack of people. When she had come with Father, they had stopped at a lot of places along the river to buy and sell. Because the river flooded, no one lived near the banks. At some places houses had been built on artificial mounds so that you could see them from the river. The houses were intact, but they saw no people. Once, they spotted a man on a horse, but he was too far away to talk to.

Three days went by like this. At night they stopped in a safe place, ate from their supplies, and slept. They would leave someone on deck as watch—usually Loesie, because she didn't seem to need any sleep at all. When Johanna came up the deck in the morning, Loesie would shake her head at the question of had she seen anyone.

Then they would harness the sea cows for another day of travel. Johanna was both keen and anxious to get to Aroden castle. Above all, she hoped that her uncle remembered who she was and that they wouldn't turn the group away once they saw Roald.

It was one thing taking Roald to Aroden. It was another expecting the Estlander royals to forget their problems with the Carmine House. The further upriver they went, the bigger and more unsurmountable they became, until she was quite certain that her uncle would order Roald hanged as soon as they entered the castle. The Estlanders hated the Carmine House. It was not for nothing that they allowed minor princesses, like Johanna's mother, to marry rich Saarlander commoners, rather than the royal family. Added to that, Estlanders spoke in a thick dialect and Johanna wasn't sure she could make herself understood.

Why didn't she think about all this before setting out?

Was there any point in going on? Maybe they should go back to see if Saardam was safe—no, that was stupid, too. The bandits wouldn't have destroyed the city and left. Saardam was such a strategic place that no one would give it up without a fight.

It was getting towards the end of the third day on the river when a whistle came from the bow of the boat.

Loesie stood at the bar handling the leather straps of the

harnesses. The sloop had stopped and drifted into a bed of reeds, where the sea cows were busily tearing up stems by the roots.

"Why have we stopped here?"

"Ghghghghgh." Loesie pointed at the horizon. Her eyes were wide.

Johanna looked.

At first she saw nothing unusual. Just an undulating field surrounded by a hedge, then a path and another field and—smoke. Jagged ruins. Her heart jumped.

"Is that Aroden?"

Loesie nodded.

The castle and the surrounding town, where her mother grew up. "Have you seen any people?"

She shook her head.

Nellie had come up behind them. "Why are we stopping here—oh!" She raised her hand to her mouth. "Is this Aroden?"

Johanna nodded. She couldn't speak. All the hope she'd had to find a safe haven fled with the sight of this destruction.

"Ghghghghghghgh." Loesie pointed up and down the river and then shrugged.

"Keep going," Johanna said.

Loesie flicked the reins to make the cows continue. The sloop slowly gathered pace. Johanna, Loesie and Nellie remained at the bow, looking over the landscape.

Around the next bend they came across more burnt-out ruins, some still smouldering. Not a thing moved, not a bird called. A waft of burnt air drifted on the wind. Oh, if only she could read the wind. Was all of Estland in ruins? Were any of her relatives still alive?

A couple of people, a woman and two young men, ran to

the riverbank, shouting. They were filthy, covered in soot. The woman had an ugly sore on her forehead.

Nellie raised her hand over her mouth. "Look at those people. What are we going to do?"

"We can't do much. We must protect Roald." Her voice wavered. She was so tired. The temptation to jump from the deck into the river was great.

"Should we moor here and check the castle?"

"I don't see that there is a point, Nellie. I'm pretty sure that burnt tower there is part of the castle. These bandits have laid the world to waste. There is no town unscathed, and if there are any royals still alive, they will be like Roald, in hiding."

A chill went over her. What if there were none left alive? What kind of chaos would descend upon the western lowlands? Many major royals had been at the ball. What if the Carmine House, the Aroden family and Baron Uti were all dead? Then Roald would be the only royal heir for all of those lands. And he would need to step up soon, so that people could have hope that peace and prosperity would return.

Neither of them said anything for a long time. The sloop moved slowly upriver and the woman and her two teenage sons slid from view. Their voices faded in the distance. Johanna felt horrible about not stopping and helping them, but with Roald on board, they couldn't afford to get involved in trouble.

It started to rain, a soft drizzle that barely made the ground wet at first, but grew more persistent. They went into the tiny cabin where Roald had spent most of his days and where it smelled uncomfortably of male sweat.

Johanna lit a candle and they shared some of their supplies. Roald chatted about cheese and ham and which kinds he liked, but no one else said much. Eventually, he fell silent as well, heaving a sigh.

"Is there anywhere your uncle could have fled to safety?" Nellie asked Johanna, her voice low.

Johanna shrugged. "The duke has a hunting lodge, but I don't know where it is." At any rate, the forests of Estland had never been the safest of places.

"What are we going to do now, Mistress Johanna?" Nellie's voice was timid.

Johanna didn't know, and felt irritated that making the decisions was all up to her.

"Maybe . . ." She stared into the flame of the candle. By its feeble light, Loesie looked wide-eyed and crazy. Johanna was no longer sure if they could trust her. Nellie's face was pale in contrast with her red and raw lips. Her bonnet was in need of a wash, and that made Johanna feel embarrassed. Nellie would normally rather die than wear something dirty.

Roald's beard had grown unruly. He looked the healthiest of all, but his mind was elsewhere.

Johanna let out a deep breath. "Let's find a place to stay for the night away from Aroden. Then tomorrow we'll see if we can turn around and go back. Maybe we can stay at Loesie's farm until we get news."

"Ghghghgh!" Loesie shook her head. She curled her fingers like claws and then made swimming movements with her hands.

Johanna frowned at her. "Do you mean that the men who attacked your farm came from across the river?"

Loesie nodded.

Across the river from Loesie's farm was the marshy no-man's land. They had passed it on the way here, but had not thought anything of it or seen anything unusual. It was a useless piece of land, inundated when it rained and too wet for forests, grazing animals or farming. Some farmers went there to cut peat, and maybe hunt ducks, but it wasn't much good for anything else. That, of course, made it good for hiding. Was that where the bandits lived?

"Do they have a leader?"

"Mmmmm." Loesie nodded. She made some hand gestures.

Johanna guessed what they meant. "He has long hair . . . He rides a horse?"

"Ghghghgh." Loesie shook her head. She pointed at the river.

"He swims?"

"Mmmm." She shook her head again and mimicked riding and pointed at the river.

"A water horse," Roald said.

Johanna frowned at him. "What is a water horse?"

"It's a creature from the fables," Nellie said. "It's a horse that has duck's feet so that it can swim."

Oh. She frowned at Loesie and again at Nellie. Did either of them believe in water horses?

"Well, it's not going to help us much now. We have to decide where to go. We could go to Lurezia for help." Because Burovia wouldn't give it, since they never liked Saarland much in the first place, and Lurezia would probably be indifferent, too far away to care.

She sighed. *Was* there even a place to go?

"We are what's left of free Saarland," Nellie said into the depressed silence.

There was nothing anyone could add to that. The free city of Saardam was dead, and Estland had been gutted. Johanna rose. She needed to be out of this smelly cabin.

It had stopped raining.

Johanna walked along the deck to the sloop's bow and sat down at the driver's bench. The sea cows were unharnessed. Their ropes dangled in the water, moving occasionally. One of the animals was chomping noisily and wetly in the dark somewhere beyond the edge of her vision.

Foggy air blanketed the riverbanks, rendering the greens of the willows and grass in muted grey. Johanna hugged herself against the cold and humid air.

Someone else came from the cabin. Nellie, judging by the sound of careful footsteps.

"Mistress Johanna? Are you all right?"

"Sit down."

Nellie settled on the bench next to her. "Oh, it's all so awful. Those poor people. I can still hear them calling out for us."

Yes, Johanna could, too. The woman and her two sons begging for help was probably an image that wouldn't leave her for the rest of her life. "Do you know we hold the freedom of Saardam in our hands? We have the only surviving member of our royal family with us. If he dies without an heir, the holding of Saardam will fall into the hands of the nearest relative, who is . . . I don't even know. Not someone who cares about us."

Horror was written on Nellie's face. Everyone knew the story of how the young Nicholaos had settled feuds that went back centuries by opening the port of Saardam for trade. Simply put, Saardam was *too important* to landlocked countries, and it suited the rival nations that a small and insignificant royal family had possession of it.

"We must find a way to take Saardam back from those bandits."

"Yes." Although that wouldn't happen until they had found other survivors.

"And Roald must have an heir as soon as possible."

"Yes." Johanna nodded, grimly. "But everyone who would be a suitable candidate for a wife is dead." The memory of the destruction of the palace made her shudder. Another image she would probably never forget.

A chill went down her back. She clamped her hands between her knees.

Nellie said, "If King Nicholaos agreed to you dancing with the prince, you are a suitable candidate."

Johanna sighed and let her shoulders slump.

Nellie began, "I'm sorry, I would have—"

"No, Nellie. I've thought about it a lot." In fact, ever since Father had mentioned the trouble of the royal family during that coach ride on their way to the ball.

"In what way did you think about it?"

Johanna thought that she had been stupid and behaved like a spoilt child that day. She didn't want to get married because marriage meant looking after a man who expected to be looked after, who expected a lady of the house who held tea parties and things like that.

Roald expected nothing of the sort. Apart from that one thing that would be unpleasant, she wasn't even sure what he expected. He seemed to be happy for her to tell him what to do. He was happy cooking. He'd been happy chopping wood. Those things he did well and efficiently. It was the talking and relationship stuff he had trouble with.

When Johanna said nothing, Nellie prompted, "Mistress Johanna? In what way?"

Johanna turned to her in the fast-waning light. "I'll protect the prince from people who only want money he doesn't have. I want to make sure that our country and our royal family stay as they are. I'll help Saarland overcome this evil and make it strong again. I will marry Roald."

CHAPTER 18

NELLIE'S FATHER was a celebrant for the Church and Nellie knew the right components of a wedding ceremony. She went into an organising frenzy. She poked Loesie into moving the sloop into a part of the river where weeping willows trailed their branches in the water.

"We'll make a nice feast out of the nicest food we have," Nellie said. Never mind that Roald would have to cook it, while she insisted on turning a farm dress into a simple wedding dress with the aid of a sheet. Nellie might be clumsy, easily flustered and impractical, but her strength was that she knew about clothes and protocol and she loved that kind of thing.

She made a table on the deck from a crate covered with a horse blanket. She went on shore to cut sprays of wild parsley flowers which she fashioned into bouquets. She set out cups and candles on the table. It was all so surreal, and it was hard to comprehend that not far away an entire town had been destroyed and its inhabitants killed or driven away.

Johanna spent most of the day sitting on top of the hold

covers watching Nellie, who was in her element and seemed to have found a shred of happiness to lift her from her misery.

They performed the ceremony on the rear deck of the barge in the waning light. Johanna wore the dress, which Nellie had made pretty with ruffles cut from one of the sheets and a necklace of flowers. Roald wore his royal jacket, which Nellie's attempt to wash had only marginally improved. The crown and the staff were hopefully still in the broom cupboard in the palace, but he still had his rings, and his fingers, although quite slender, were thicker than hers. His seal.

Nellie slid the golden ring on Johanna's index finger, the only finger it would fit. It felt heavy and cumbersome on her hand.

Roald stood stiff and wouldn't look at anyone.

Johanna was scared, cold and miserable and shivered through most of it, but inside her, she felt a seed of pride. She held herself straight while Nellie spoke all the words she had heard her father say so many times.

She was nervous, too, and stumbled a few times.

Johanna did this for her country, for the freedom of Saardam. If the four of them were all that was left of the free kingdom, then the four of them would do their best to find other free people and liberate their country.

Johanna didn't know that Roald understood much of Nellie's words. He stared at the riverbank most of the time, and had to be prompted to make his reply.

"I do," sounded like a death sentence coming from those lifeless lips.

They went inside the cabin, and ate some of the best

sausages Johanna and Roald had collected from the farm, drank the wine from the captain's cabin, but it was not until Nellie said that from now on Johanna and Roald should have the captain's cabin, that it fully hit what she'd agreed to do. And she thought at that moment Roald understood, too. All of a sudden, she was overcome by the desire to scream at Nellie *don't leave me alone with him,* but it was far too late. Nellie announced that she was tired and she and Loesie left.

Johanna stood there in the middle of the cabin, clamping her hands around her as Roald shut the door, and bolted it. No way out.

"We are married, now?" he asked.

"Yes."

He laughed, "Heheheheeee." His eyes twinkled with mischief. "Now I can look."

Johanna cringed, but there was really no way out, and the quicker this part was over and done with, the better.

Slowly she opened the buttons of her dress and pulled the fabric aside. He sat on the edge of the bed as she wrestled herself out of her dress. Watching. She was so nervous he could have knocked her over with a single finger. He just sat and watched, his eyes wide, as she hung up the dress and slid her underclothes off, first the underdress, and then the corset. The hooks came undone; her breasts hung free. His mouth fell open, like a little boy in a sweet store. She didn't think he had seen a naked woman before.

With great effort, she had to force herself to cross to him. She slid the jacket off his shoulders. With a feeling of shame, she noticed that it was still not completely dry.

"Come."

She had to force herself not to shudder. Her fingers trembled as she undid his shirt. His skin underneath was soft and quite tanned, completely without chest hair, and so skinny that his ribs were clearly visible. His nipples, dark brown and erect, lay flat against his chest. No man-boobs here. Apart from his tan, he didn't look very healthy. How often did he forget to eat?

The trousers were harder to get off and not just because she was nervous or unfamiliar with the belt buckle and fastening. He bent over to stroke her naked shoulders very gingerly with the tips of his fingers, making goose bumps run down her back. His hands were cold.

The belt fell off and the trousers came down. He undid the string to his under pants. They fell, too, but remained suspended on a particular part of his anatomy. He grinned.

"I'm a man, see? I know what to do."

She doubted it. She didn't know herself. For all the flirting and the dancing she had done, the kiss from the Baron's son was the closest she'd ever come to the marital bed and that bed loomed ever closer against the back wall of the cabin. The curtains fluttered with a draught.

She sat next to him on the edge of the mattress, the sheets soft under her naked skin.

He sat next to her and cupped her breast in his hand, a skinny, bony hand with large knuckles.

"It's so soft." His chest heaved with deep breaths. His eyes, wide and mad, were on the hair between her legs. "Hee hee heeee. I know what to do," he said.

With one hand, he pushed her down in the mattress. Johanna forced herself to recline willingly. Best not to resist, lest he go into one of his aggressive moods. Blood roared in her ears.

With surprising agility, he jumped on her and pushed her back into the pillows. Naked skin met naked skin. His was clammy, and slick with sweat. He thrust his hips forward, hard, and his member poked painfully into a very sensitive spot. She couldn't restrain a yelp.

"Ow!"

He ignored her and kept pushing, now rocking his hips. She tried spreading her legs, but he was all over the place, smearing slime on her inner thighs.

"Roald, stop. Stop!"

He did, which surprised her, his chest heaving.

"You're hurting me." She was shivering so much that her jaw threatened to seize up. "Maybe it's better if you lie on your back."

"All right." He chuckled.

She clambered off the narrow bunk and waited, trying to get control of her shattered nerves while he settled himself. A wide grin spread across his face.

She stepped closer to the bed. He grabbed her wrist and pulled her. Johanna almost fell on top of him.

"Wait, calm down."

She lifted her leg over him and crouched over him. This bunk sure wasn't made for these types of acrobatics. "Here," she whispered, while holding his member up. The tip glistered with slime. "Hold it like that."

She lowered herself, found the right spot. Breathed in deeply, pushed down. There was a sharp pain and tightness as he slid into her.

He gave a long moan, his head arched back into the pillow.

Well, that was it, she guessed. She was no longer a virgin. But what now? This wasn't "it", was it?

She slowly rocked her hips. He moaned again and gripped her thighs with white-knuckled hands, arched his back so he lifted her right off the mattress.

"Ow, ow. That's hurts!"

But he was bucking and threshing like wild sea cow in a net and Johanna was being bounced about. She managed to get her knees under her, and lifted herself at the same time he arched his back. He slipped out of her.

"Wait, Roald."

But he bucked and emitted a loud "Huuuuhhhh!" and something wet squirted over her right thigh.

He fell back onto the pillow. Johanna sat there, trembling, while she watched a glob of white slime trickle down her leg.

She guessed *that* was it, and it hadn't quite gone where it was intended to go.

"That was good," he said. "I want more."

He stared up at the ceiling. His member had already gone limp. She didn't think there would be 'more' tonight.

She was shivering so much she could barely lift herself from the bed. Her upper legs were a sticky mess and when she felt the sore spot between her legs, her finger came away covered in blood-streaked slime.

There was nothing in the cabin to wipe herself and she didn't want to go outside like this. Nellie would . . .

Oh, Nellie.

The cabin faded in a haze of tears.

Johanna managed to get her underdress back on and lay down in the warm hollow in the mattress next to him. He was asleep in moments. Johanna cried into the pillow all night.

CHAPTER 19

THE NEXT MORNING she clambered from the bed sore and feeling dirty.

Roald was still asleep and she intended to leave him that way. What if he wanted to do it again? She didn't think she could face that.

She wrestled herself into her other clothes and went on deck.

Nellie stood there, her hands crossed over her chest, while Loesie threw carrots at the sea cows.

Oh holy Triune. Not another fight.

"She wanted to disturb you." Nellie glared at Loesie, who poked out her tongue.

"She could have knocked. I was awake." Johanna found it hard to keep discomfort out of her voice. She couldn't meet Nellie's eyes. There were just too many questions hovering within. She would have heard Roald's grunts last night.

"I wouldn't let her disturb anyone on the morning after their wedding. The union between man and woman is holy—"

Johanna waved her to silence. *Don't talk nonsense, Nellie.*

Tears threatened in her eyes.

Everything hurt, every step she took. In her mind, she still heard Roald give that horrible grunt when he spilled himself. That must have echoed all over the ship.

"Mistress Johanna? Are you all right? Do you want to sit down?"

Johanna glared at Nellie, her wide eyes, her pale face.

What did she think? That the future of the kingdom grew inside her? That she needed mollycoddling because of that? It couldn't even be so, and what was worse, she would have to endure Roald's attentions until it did. What did she know?

She wanted to laugh, and cry and slap her in the face.

"Don't say that to me again."

"Mistress Johanna?"

She whirled at her. "Stop calling me that. Call me Johanna, or call me nothing at all, instead of treating me like a. . . ." Her voice cracked.

Nellie shrank back, her chest heaving, and said nothing for a long time. Johanna stared out over the water, wiping stubborn tears from her cheeks.

"But Mi . . . er . . . Johanna, you *are* the queen now and I will treat you like that." She dipped a curtsey and Johanna had an even greater desire to punch her in the face.

"Please, Nellie."

Roald's ring felt like a millstone on her hand. Like this, it was so visible, and it was too big for her. She took off her necklace, slid the ring off and threaded the necklace through. When she did it back up again, the ring hung between her breasts.

"It's too big. I'm afraid I might lose it."

Nellie nodded.

"Let's just go and see what Loesie wants. If she wanted to disturb me, that means she has something to say."

She went to the bow, but Loesie was no longer there. She stood on the riverbank, her hand on the trunk of a willow tree. People in these parts didn't cut willows, and its branches trailed in the water. Soft green misted the pale wood. Spring came.

"Loesie?" Johanna called.

She looked up and gestured *come*.

The current had brought the boat right into shore. There was an old jetty here and they didn't need the dinghy to clamber out, but the section where it joined up to the shore had collapsed. Johanna took off her shoes and waded through the water to the small sandy beach.

She joined Loesie at the tree trunk. Soft branches brushed over her head, and bees buzzed amongst the little furry balls that were the willow's flowers.

"Anything here?" she asked.

Loesie took her hand and pulled it to the rough wood of the tree trunk.

The green riverbank faded. It was dusk, and a long procession of men on large horses followed the river downstream. Horses and spears and fur jerkins.

"Who are they?" she asked Loesie.

She shook her head. *Ghghghgh.* She pointed up the bank.

They left the shelter of the branches of the tree. Nellie had just come ashore and was wrestling her shoes back onto her feet.

"What's going on?" she asked. Her cheeks were red and flustered. Brilliant sunlight brought out the greens and yellows of the meadow. The top of the riverbank led into an orchard, the trees full of white flowers.

Large daisies bloomed in the grass between the trees, and purple and pink flowers, so different from what Johanna had ever seen.

Nellie was the first one in the meadow. "Isn't this pretty?" She already had a handful of flowers. "We can make you a more cheerful wedding bouquet."

Johanna cringed. "Let's be careful." An orchard usually meant that there was a farmhouse nearby.

"I'm not doing any harm." Nellie continued picking. "If I don't pick flowers, they're going to get eaten by those cows over there."

The cows were grey-brown, very unlike the black and white ones that were common with farmers in Saarland. There was a group of four or five of them in the shade of a tree.

A rutted track led out of the orchard. It disappeared along a bend behind a mass of dark trees.

A pine forest.

A chill crept over Johanna's back. She heard the voices in the wind whistling through the boughs. She felt the tingle of magic that tugged at her senses but showed her nothing because she didn't have wind magic. "Maybe we should return to the *Lady Sara*." Roald was there alone.

"In a moment. When I've got all the flowers I need."

It was the first time that she had seen Nellie being her old self, so Johanna calmed her nerves and sat down in the grass. The scent of crushed herbs rose up to her. The sunlight was warm and comfortable, the meadow a kaleidoscope of cheerful colours. She was just making herself scared by thinking about magic. Likely there was nothing to be afraid of once you got used to the sounds of the forest.

She glanced at Loesie, but she had also sat down and stared into the distance with a dreamy look.

Guess a little rest was all right.

She lay back in the grass.

The next thing she knew, she woke up with the sound of a cow chomping on leaves.

What?

"Nellie, what . . ." She sat up with a jerk. Nellie lay behind her, her head resting on her elbow. Her eyes were closed and her chest moved in regular breaths. A bunch of wilted flowers lay next to her.

"Loesie?"

The field was empty. Loesie was nowhere to be seen.

Nellie opened her eyes. "Oh, pardon me, Mistress Johanna. I think I fell asleep."

"We all fell asleep. The past few days have been tiring for all of us. I guess we earned the rest."

"Look at my poor flowers! I must get some new ones."

"We need to go back. I don't know what Loesie and Roald have been up to, but they must be wondering where we are."

Nellie looked disappointed, but didn't protest.

They walked back over the hill, between the blooming apple trees. Then down the bank to the *Lady Sara* which lay bobbing peacefully, with the roaming lines of the sea cows attached. The animals were grazing on the bottom. Loesie was nowhere to be seen.

Johanna and Nellie waded through the water to the half-rotten and wobbly jetty.

When Johanna was halfway up the ladder to the deck, a dark silhouette appeared at the top. Someone that was not Roald, but a much bigger man with a ponytail.

She gasped but she had nowhere to go. Nellie was behind her and couldn't go down quickly enough. Not only that, two more bandits waded towards them from the shore.

Nellie screamed.

The thug on the deck grabbed Johanna's arm and yanked her up onto the deck. There were not one but three thugs on the deck—all of them bearded and with long-furred jerkins. Two wore ponytails; the third and biggest thug was bald. They laughed when their mate dumped Johanna onto the deck. Behind her, Nellie was struggling against the grip of one of the men who had come up behind them, screaming and kicking.

"Let us go. We're free citizens of Saarland." Johanna straightened herself and tried to sound impressive, as if . . . Roald. Where was Roald?

The men laughed and exchanged comments in a strange and harsh-sounding language. One of the men was tying Nellie's hands up with a dirty rag. Nellie was still kicking at the man, and in response, he grabbed the front of her dress and thrust a hand down.

Nellie screamed.

"Stop it, Nellie. The more you protest, the more they like it. Keep still." *And you might just come out of here alive.* Although maybe not unscathed.

A sixth man now clambered up from the hold, with Loesie over his shoulder. She was pulling his hair, but he set her down as if she didn't exist. Great bundles of hair hung from her hands.

Johanna still couldn't see Roald anywhere. What if they . . . The ring under her shirt felt heavy. If Roald was dead, then . . .

Panic rose in her. If that was true, then the whole future of free Saarland was in her hands.

Then, she heard splashing and growling and yet another thug came up the ladder, pulling Roald with him. Water dripped from his clothes, his hair standing on end on one side of his head.

The men laughed.

Roald's eyes were as wide as Johanna had seen them that day when they fished him out of the harbour. Any moment now and he'd start banging his head on something.

The thug pushed Roald forward to the railing as if he wanted to throw him off the boat. Roald squealed.

"Keep your hands off him," Johanna yelled.

The men laughed again. One pushed Roald harder into the railing. But then the bald one shouted something, and they let Roald go. He fell heavily on his backside. "They'll kill us. They'll kill us!" His squeal chilled Johanna deeply. "They'll kill us. They'll kill us!"

"Shhh, calm down."

Roald met her eyes, and some of the madness seeped out of his face.

The bald-headed bandit leader jerked his head towards the riverbank.

There, on the high bank, approached three more men with a whole team of huge horses black as night. They had long flowing manes and huge hooves. With them were two bears on chains and a pack of dogs.

The bald leader yelled something, and a voice responded from the bank. The group descended to the water, the horses snorting and blowing, tossing their great heads. Some of them waded a bit into the water. The bears appeared nervous, pulling on their chains.

The bandits forced Johanna, Nellie and Roald to clamber down the ladder, and wade through the water.

Johanna sat down to take off her shoes, but a thug pulled her up. Nellie cried when they pushed her down the jetty. "Do you know how much those shoes cost my father?"

The only thing she got in response was more rough handling.

On the riverbank, the bandits hauled each of them in front of another rider on a horse.

Johanna's horse was smelly and the man at her back stank of sweat and chewing tobacco. He snaked an arm around her waist, but she pushed him away. She would not let herself be humiliated.

"I can ride myself. You don't have to hold me."

She glanced at Roald, gave him her best *behave like a king* glare, and said, "Sit up."

He did. His face was so pale that she was afraid that he

might faint. Hopefully he would remain quiet about who he was.

The bald leader whistled and the column of horses set off, away from the riverbank, into the forest. Johanna cast a look over her shoulder to where the *Lady Sara* lay. She had to remember this place. One day, she would come back.

THANK YOU

For reading Innocence Lost. The story continues with Willow Witch, in which our friends are taken through ghost and demon-filled woods to face dangers of a magical kind.

ABOUT THE AUTHOR

Patty Jansen lives in Sydney, Australia, where she spends most of her time writing Science Fiction and Fantasy.

Her story *This Peaceful State of War* placed first in the second quarter of the Writers of the Future contest and was published in their 27th anthology. She has also sold fiction to genre magazines such as Analog Science Fiction and Fact, Redstone SF and Aurealis.

Patty has written over twenty novels in both Science Fiction and Fantasy, including the *Icefire Trilogy* and the *Ambassador* series.

pattyjansen.com

BOOKS BY PATTY JANSEN

MORE INFORMATION:

PATTYJANSEN.COM

9 781925 841633